CHARLOTTE BRONTË

STANCLIFFE'S HOTEL

EDITED BY HEATHER GLEN

PENGUIN BOOKS

PENGUIN BOOKS

Published by the Penguin Group
Penguin Books Ltd, 80 Strand, London WC2R ORL, England
Penguin Putnam Inc., 375 Hudson Street, New York, New York 10014, USA
Penguin Books Australia Ltd, 250 Camberwell Road, Camberwell, Victoria 3124, Australia
Penguin Books Canada Ltd, 10 Alcorn Avenue, Toronto, Ontario, Canada M4V 3B2
Penguin Books India (P) Ltd, 11 Community Centre, Panchsheel Park, New Delhi – 110 017, India
Penguin Books (NZ) Ltd, Cnr Rosedale and Airborne Roads, Albany, Auckland, New Zealand
Penguin Books (South Africa) (Pty) Ltd, 24 Sturdee Avenue, Rosebank 2196, South Africa

Penguin Books Ltd, Registered Offices: 80 Strand, London WC2R ORL, England

www.penguin.com

First published 2003

4

Editorial material copyright © Heather Glen, 2003
Text reproduced courtesy of The Brontë Parsonage Museum
All rights reserved

The moral right of the editor has been asserted

Set in Adobe Sabon
Typeset by Rowland Phototypesetting Ltd, Bury St Edmunds, Suffolk
Printed in England by Clays Ltd, St Ives plc

Contents

Preface

Charlotte Brontë is known to readers today as the author of *Jane Eyre*, one of the most popular novels in the English literary canon. More than 150 years after its first publication, it is still the third most borrowed volume in English public libraries. The story of the Brontë sisters' brief lives is almost as well known. Indeed, their home, Haworth Parsonage, has become one of the most visited of England's literary shrines. It may therefore seem surprising that the novelette which follows has never before been published; that until now, its material existence has consisted of 34 small pages, 11.5 × 19 cm in size, crammed with a fading, handwritten 'print' so tiny that it is almost impossible to decipher without the aid of a magnifying glass. But if only a handful of scholars has hitherto read this story (for example, Christine Alexander, who included it in her unpublished 1979 thesis on Brontë's early writings), the reason lies less, perhaps, in the difficulties presented by the manuscript, than in the strangeness of the world of which it speaks.

When Elizabeth Gaskell was beginning work on her *Life of Charlotte Brontë*, she came upon 'a curious packet ..., containing an immense amount of manuscript, in an inconceivably small space' – the equivalent, her husband suggested, of '50 volumes of print'. She had stumbled upon the records of the kingdom of Glass Town, first created by the four young

Brontës when Charlotte, the eldest, was thirteen. For the story of the Brontë family was not simply one of tragedy, the loss of their mother, and isolation. For nearly twenty years before the appearance of *Jane Eyre*, the parsonage at Haworth was a place of lively creative activity. Together, these gifted children had constructed a whole imaginary world, with its own geography, politics and dramatis personae – the latter modelled at first on real-life public figures (writers, artists, statesmen, explorers) but gradually evolving into completely fictional characters. Emily and Anne had soon broken off to create their own country of Gondal, but Branwell and Charlotte went on with the Glass Town saga, producing dozens of miniature novels, poems and imitation journals, purported to be written by their protagonists. Gaskell was baffled by this 'wild weird writing', which seemed to her to give evidence of 'creative power carried to the verge of insanity'. She provided her readers with a facsimile of a page to demonstrate its 'extreme minuteness', and dismissed it all in her biography as intelligible only to 'the bright little minds for whom it was intended', a 'curious' phenomenon of childhood, hardly to be taken seriously.

But the Brontës had in fact continued their 'plays' (as they called them) throughout adolescence and beyond. Emily and Anne were writing books about Gondal at 27 and 25. Charlotte and Branwell transferred their interest (and many of their characters) to the new kingdom of Angria, and were still, in their early twenties, adding to it both in poetry and in prose. The manuscripts of the Gondal saga have all disappeared, but many of the Angrian writings survive, equalling in volume all of the Brontës' published works.

Like the earliest Glass Town writings, the later Angrian stories are not autobiographical. Their narrators and their protagonists are the dramatis personae of Angria – as Charlotte put it, in a journal fragment, those 'many well known forms ... faces looking up, eyes smiling and lips moving in audible speech, that I knew better almost than my brother and sisters, yet whose voices had never woke an echo in this world'. And they are not exactly juvenilia, but works of maturity. The Charlotte Brontë who wrote them was not a novice author, but one whose 'apprenticeship in writing' (as she was later to call it) had lasted for a number of years. She was, moreover, writing for a sophisticated audience, albeit a tiny one. Although the Brontë family were isolated, they were avid readers not merely of poetry and fiction but of newspapers and journals, extraordinarily alert to the literary, linguistic and cultural life of their time. Since childhood they had been responding to, parodying, criticizing one another's work. It was within this lively context that *Stancliffe's Hotel* was written, one of a number of 'plays' produced by Charlotte and Branwell in 1837–9.

Like the other Angrian manuscripts, *Stancliffe's Hotel* was written for an audience familiar with the 'plays'. Present-day readers, however, will need at least an outline to understand the landscape, politics and history of the world which it depicts. Angria lay to the east of the Glass Town Federation. It was divided into seven provinces, each with a capital city and a Lord Lieutenant; its king was the Duke of Zamorna, who had evolved out of Arthur Wellesley, the eldest son of the Duke of Wellington, the increasingly prominent hero of the earlier Glass Town 'plays'. Whereas those 'plays' had been set in exotic Africa, the landscape of Angria is recognizably English. It has moors and forests and great country houses; the city of Zamorna, with its 'Piece-hall', mills and Stancliffe's Hotel bustling with commercial travellers, is like a thriving early industrial Yorkshire town. To the west lies 'Senegambia', a country rather like Ireland, original homeland both of Zamorna and Mary Percy, his second wife.

At the centre of the Angrian drama, as Charlotte Brontë conceives it (and in the background of *Stancliffe's Hotel*, prompting the street-riot in Zamorna City), is the love/hate relationship between two men. The younger of these is Zamorna, a darkly handsome Byronic figure, charismatic, ruthless, unfaithful to a series of mistresses and wives. The other is the Earl of Northangerland, father of Mary Percy, once Zamorna's ally, and subsequently leader of a rebellion against him. In the course of that rebellion, Angria was devastated by war, and Zamorna driven into exile. By the time of *Stancliffe's Hotel* he has been re-established in power, and the ill and ageing Northangerland is confined to his country estate. Yet the bond between them has not been broken, as Zamorna's visit to him in this story attests.

Stancliffe's Hotel is very different from *Jane Eyre*. The narrator is not a central, passionately involved protagonist, but a detached, debunking observer of Angrian life and manners, Charles Townshend, a dandy who takes 'a full half hour to dress, and another half hour to view myself over from head to foot'. This is not a suspenseful story which rushes the reader to conclusion, but a succession of vignettes. 'Sketches' such as these were a feature of the writing of the 1830s – expressive, it has been argued, of a new kind of urban experience: Dickens's *Sketches by Boz* had been published in 1836. Here, the sense is of a fictional world too protean to be presented in a single linear narrative, a series of snapshots of a larger reality that can be viewed from different perspectives and in very different ways. There are sudden changes of scene, marked by gaps in the manuscript; shifts of tone and atmosphere; tensions are left unresolved. Yet the feeling is not of fragmentariness but of telling juxtaposition: flexible, witty, assured.

For the structure of *Stancliffe's Hotel* is not quite as inconsequential as it looks. If it is offered as a series of disconnected episodes, it seems to have been conceived as a whole. It begins with Louisa Dance affectedly quoting Byron, and ends with Zamorna and his wife reading Byron together. But what one finds in this 'novelette' (as its author half mockingly called it) is less that heroic romanticism sometimes attributed to Byron than his undercutting irony. In the opening scene Charles Townshend's cool view of the ecstasies of his 'fair companion' is succeeded by the debunking image of Macara stupefied by opium. Jane Moore's stirring song of remembered valour in battle is sardonically echoed in Townshend's later description of Lord Stuartville's rather less glorious charge on the 'mad mechanics and desperate operatives of Zamorna': not a battle, but a 'frightful scene'. What should be climactic moments of masculine assertion or triumph either do not happen or end in discomfiture.

Charlotte Brontë, who is still often thought of as writing only of women's experience, seems here more critically concerned with masculinity. Where Branwell's writings of this period are full of descriptions of battles, Sir William Percy in *Stancliffe's Hotel* boasts of his own exploits by quoting from the newspapers, but is also comically aware of the fashionable figure he strikes. The episode at the centre in which the two young dandies, Townshend and William Percy, pursue 'the Rose of Zamorna' ends in their being cut down to size. 'Two chits,' says she. Even Zamorna is portrayed with a certain irony, taking snuff in a carriage in the midst of a hostile crowd, sitting 'like any wet Quaker whom the spirit had not yet moved'. Through it all runs the deflating voice of the cynical Townshend, a half-ridiculous figure: watching the riot from the second storey, 'twenty persons . . . at my back, pressing one behind another to get a glimpse from the window'; voyeuristically describing the final tableau in the bedroom where, in the company of her troubling husband, who is 'for aught she knew, faithful', the Duchess tries to find peace.

This is an emphatically unheroic and unromantic world. The only military glory appears in a song in a drawing-room; the only 'heroes' described are a 'calvacade' of manufacturers returning from dinner on market-day, 'safe in the external shield of waterproof capes and the internal specific of no less waterproof cognac'; the only 'reveille' that of a 'thrilling voice'. Here instead there are newspapers with fashionable gossip columns, and thriving, bustling trade – an inn full of vociferous commercial travellers, a street with a 'splendid mercer's shop . . . waving streamers of silk and print pendant to the shop door', a mill-chimney 'whose cylindrical pillar rose three hundred feet into the air'. The characters eat and drink a good deal: 'hot punch and oysters for supper', 'rice-currie, devilled turkey and guava', 'proof spirits' and 'watered Hollands', 'salmagundi', 'roast chicken and oyster-sauce'. Charlotte Brontë has a sharp eye for the latest in dress fashions: Louisa wears a 'boa' (a word first used in 1836); Townshend (more mystifyingly to the twenty-first-century reader) 'a well-made green frock and light summer jeans' (a frock-coat and trousers made of coarse cotton cloth). And she has a sharp ear too for contemporary slang phrases (and worse): 'Drat it'; 'Go it old cock!'; 'These Angrians do lavish the blunt' (throw money about); 'prigging' (stealing); 'stived up' (suffocated); 'the old harlot-ridden buck'. If this story is set in Angria, its language and concerns are those of the England of the 1830s: the England of dandies and silver fork novels, in which the aspiring middle classes ape the fashions of the aristocracy and the glories of Lord Wellington's victories are only a distant dream.

Stancliffe's Hotel will be of enormous interest to those who know Charlotte Brontë only as the author of *Jane Eyre*. Racier than anything she published in her lifetime, full of comic and haunting vignettes, experimental in form, it offers a suggestive challenge to the popular sense of Charlotte as an artless transcriber of her own experience into fiction, and affords an indispensable insight into this extraordinary writer's work.

Note on the Text

The manuscript of *Stancliffe's Hotel* is in The Brontë Parsonage Museum, Haworth. It is erratically punctuated, mainly with dashes, and has very little paragraphing, though there are gaps in the manuscript to mark changes of scene. For the convenience of the present-day reader, I have modernized punctuation, capitalization and hyphenation, and introduced paragraphs. In several cases, where a word or part of a word seems to have been left out of the manuscript, it has been added in square brackets. Obvious spelling mistakes have been silently corrected, but archaic spellings have been preserved.

Dramatis Personae

The action takes place late in the Angrian saga, when the age-ing Northangerland, who has led an unsuccessful rebellion against his son-in-law Zamorna, lies ill on his country estate at Alnwick.

Dance, Louisa Opera-singer who married Zamorna's uncle, the Marquis of Wellesley, and later a Mr Vernon. She became mistress of Northangerland during his rebellion against Zamorna, and bore him a daughter, Caroline Vernon, who is the subject of a later novelette. At the time of *Stancliffe's Hotel*, she is mistress of Macara Lofty.

Enara, General Henri Fernando di Lord Lieutenant of the Province of Etrei.

Hartford, Lord Edward General in the Angrian army.

Lofty, Lord Macara One of Northangerland's former allies.

Moore, Jane Angrian society beauty.

Northangerland Alexander Percy, Earl of Northangerland, father-in-law of Zamorna, once his ally and Prime Minister, then leader of the Republican Party, which attempted to displace him.

Percy, Edward Eldest son of Northangerland, a leading industrialist in Angria.

Percy, Mary Henrietta Northangerland's daughter and Zamorna's second wife, Duchess of Zamorna.

Percy, Sir William Second son of the Earl of Northangerland, half-brother to Mary Percy. A foppish young man.

Richton Sir John Flower, Viscount Richton, Verdopolitan Ambassador to Angria.

Rowley, Hannah Housekeeper at Charles Townshend's lodgings.

Stuartville, Earl of Viscount Castlereagh, Lord Lieutenant of the Province of Zamorna.

Surena, Mr Charles Townshend's landlord, a shopkeeper in Verdopolis.

Thornton, General Sir Wilson Bluff Yorkshireman, Lord Lieutenant of the Province of Calabar, married to Zamorna's cousin, Julia Wellesley.

Townshend, Charles Evolved, in the Angrian saga, from Lord Charles Florian Wellesley, younger brother of Zamorna. A cynical young dandy, narrator of *Stancliffe's Hotel*.

Warner, Warner Howard Successor to Northangerland as Prime Minister of Angria.

Zamorna Arthur Augustus Adrian, Duke of Zamorna and King of Angria, a charismatic, amoral, Byronic figure, who is the hero of Charlotte Brontë's Glass Town and Angrian writings.

Stancliffe's Hotel

Charles Townshend pays a visit to Louisa Dance's house, and finds Macara Lofty under the influence of opium

'Amen!' Such was the sound, given in a short shout, which closed the evening service at Ebenezer Chapel. Mr Bromley rose from his knees. He had wrestled hard, and the sweat of his pious labours shone like oil upon his forehead. Fetching a deep breath and passing his handkerchief over his damp brow, the apostle sank back in his seat. Then, extending both brawny arms and resting them on the sides of the pulpit, with the yellow-spotted handkerchief dependent from one hand, he sat and watched the evacuation of the crowded galleries.

'How oppressively hot the chapel has been to-night,' said a soft voice to me, and a bonnet, bending forward, waved its ribbons against my face.

'Aye, in two senses,' was my answer. 'Literally, as to atmosphere, and figuratively, as to zeal. Our brother has exercised[1] with freedom, madam.'

'Nonsense, Charles! I never can get into this slang! But come, the crowd is lessening at the gallery-door. I think we shall be able to make our way through it now, and I do long to get a breath of fresh air. Give me my shawl, Charles.'

The lady rose, and, while I carefully enveloped her in the shawl and boa which were to protect her from the night-air, she said, smiling persuasively, 'You will escort me to my villa and sup with me on a radish and an egg.' I answered by pressing the white hand over which she was just drawing a glove of French kid. She passed that hand through my arm and we left the gallery together.

A perfectly still and starlight night welcomed us as we quitted the steam and torches of the chapel. Threading our way quickly through the dispersing crowd at the door, we entered a well-known and oft-trod way, which in half an hour brought us from among the lighted shops and busy streets of our *quartier* to the deep shade and – at this hour – the unbroken retirement of the vale.

'Charles,' said my fair companion in her usual voice, half a whisper, half a murmur. 'Charles, what a sweet night – a premature summer night! It only wants the moon to make it perfect – then I could see my villa. Those stars are not close enough to bring out the white front fully from its laurels. And yet I do see a light glittering there. Is it not from my drawing-room window?'

'Probably,' was my answer, and I said no more. Her ladyship's softness is at times too surfeiting, more especially when she approaches the brink of the sentimental.

'Charles,' she pursued, in no wise abashed by my coolness. 'How many fond recollections come on us at such a time as this! Where do you think my thoughts always stray on a summer night? What image do you think "a cloudless clime and starry skies" always suggests?'

'Perhaps,' said I, 'that of the most noble Richard, Marquis of Wellesley, as you last saw him, reposing in gouty chair and stool, with eyelids gently closed by the influence of the pious libations in claret with which he has concluded the dinner of rice-currie, devilled turkey and guava.'

Louisa, instead of being offended, laughed with silver sound. 'You are partly right,' said she. 'The figure you have described does indeed form a portion of my recollections. Now, will you finish the picture, or shall I do it in your stead?'

'I resign the pencil into hands better qualified for its management,' rejoined I.

'Well, then, listen,' continued the Marchioness. 'Removed from the easy chair and cushioned foot-stool and from the slumbering occupant thereof, imagine a harp – that very harp which stands now in my boudoir. Imagine a woman, seated by it. I need not describe her: it is myself. She is not playing. She is listening to one who leans on her instrument and whispers as softly as the wind now whispers in my acacias.'

'Hem!' said I. 'Is the figure that of a bald elderly gentleman?'

Louisa sighed her affirmative.

'By the bye,' continued I. 'It is constantly reported that he has taken to –'

'What?' interrupted the Marchioness. 'Not proof spirits, I hope! Watered Hollands I know scarcely satisfied him.'

'No, madam, repress your fears. I was alluding merely to his dress. The pantaloons are gone: he sports white tights and silks.'

Low as the whisper was in which I communicated these stunning tidings, it thrilled along Louisa's nerves to her heart. During the pause which followed, I waited in breathless expectation for the effect. It came at last. Tittering faintly, she exclaimed, 'You don't say so! Lord! how odd! But after all, I think it's judicious, you know. Nothing can exhibit more perfect symmetry than his leg, and then he does get older of course, and a change of costume was becoming advisable. Yet I should almost fear there would be too much spindle, he was very thin, you know – very –'

'Have you heard from his lordship lately?' I asked.

'Oh no! About six months ago I had indeed one little note, but I gave it to Macara by mistake, and really I don't know what became of it afterwards.'

'Did Macara express hot sentiment of incipient jealousy on thus accidentally learning that you had not entirely dropped all correspondence with the noble Earl?'

'Yes. He said he thought the note was very civilly expressed, and wished me to answer it in terms equally polite.'

'Good! And you did so?'

'Of course. I penned an elegant billet on a sheet of rose-tinted note-paper, and sealed it with a pretty green seal bearing the device of twin hearts consumed by the same flame. Some misunderstanding must have occurred, though, for in two or three days afterwards I received it back unopened and carefully enclosed in a cover. The direction was not in his lordship's hand-writing: Macara told me he thought it was the Countess's.'

'Do you know Selden House, where his lordship now resides?' I asked.

'Ah yes! Soon after I was married I remember passing it while on a bridal excursion to Rossland[2] with the old

4

Marquis. We took lunch there, indeed, for Colonel Selden (at that time the owner of it) was a friend of my venerable bridegroom's. Talking of those times reminds me of a mistake everybody was sure to make at the hotels and private houses etc. where we stopped. I was universally taken for Lord Wellesley's daughter. Colonel Selden in particular persisted in calling me Lady Julia. He was a fine-looking man, not so old as my illustrious spouse by at least twenty years. I asked Dance, who accompanied us on that tour, why he had not chosen for me such a partner as the gallant Colonel. He answered me by the sourest look I ever saw.'

'Well,' said I, interrupting her ladyship's reminiscences. 'Here we are at your villa. Goodnight. I cannot sup with you this evening: I am engaged.'

'Nay, Charles,' returned she, retaining the hand I would have withdrawn from hers. 'Do come in! It is so long since I have had the pleasure of a quiet tète à tète with you.'

I persisted for some time in my refusal; but at length yielding to the smile and the soft tone of entreaty I gave up the point, and followed the Marchioness in.

On entering her ladyship's parlour, we found the candles lighted and a supper-tray placed ready for us on the table. By the hearth, alone, Lord Macara Lofty was seated. His hand, drooping over the arm-chair, held two open letters: his eyes were fixed on the fire – as seemed, in thought. Louisa roused him. I could not help being struck by the languid gaze with which he turned his eyes upon her as she bent over him. There was vacancy in his aspect, and dreamy stupor.

5

'Are we late from chapel?' said she. 'Bromley's last prayer seemed interminably long.'

'Rather, I should think,' was the Viscount's answer. 'Rather, a trifle or so – late, you said? O ah! to be sure. I have been sitting with you two hours, have I not Louisa? – just dusk when I walked up the valley – late! certainly –'

This not particularly intelligible reply was given in the tone and with the manner of a man just startled from a heavy slumber, and yet the noble Viscount had evidently been wide awake when we entered the room. Having delivered the speech above mentioned, he ceased to notice the Marchioness, and relapsed as if involuntarily into his former position and look.

'Won't you take some supper?' she inquired.

No answer. She repeated the question.

'G—d, no,' he said hastily, as if annoyed at interruption, his countenance at the same time wearing a rapt expression, as if every faculty were spell-bound in some absorbing train of thought. The Marchioness turned from him with a grimace. She nodded at me and whispered,

'Learned men now and then have very strange vagaries.'

Not at all discomposed by his strange conduct, she proceeded quietly to remove her bonnet, shawl and boa; and having thrown them over the back of a sofa, she passed her fingers through her hair, and shaking aside the loose ringlets into which it was thus parted, turned towards the mirror a face by no means youthful, by no means blooming, by no means regularly beautiful – but which yet had been able, by the aid of that long chiselled nose, those soft and sleepy eyes, and that bland smile always hovering round the deceitful lips, to captivate the greatest man of his age.

'Come,' she said, gliding towards the table. 'Take a sandwich, Charles, and give me a wing of that chicken. We can amuse each other till Macara thinks proper to come round and behave like a sensible Christian.'

I did not, reader, ask what was the matter with Macara, for I had a very good guess myself as to the cause and origin of that profound fit of meditation in which his lordship now sat entranced. I fell forthwith to the discussion of the sandwiches and chicken, which the Marchioness dispensed to me with liberal hand. She also sat, and, as we sipped wine together, her soft eyes looking over the brim of the glass expressed far more easy enjoyment of the good things given her for her use than perplexing concern for the singular quandary in which her *cher ami* sat speechless and motionless by the hearth. Meantime, the ecstatic smiles which had, every now and then, kindled Macara's eye and passed like sunshine over his countenance began to recur with fainter effect and at longer intervals. The almost sensual look of intense gratification and absorption gave place to an air of fatigue. Our voices seemed recalling him to recollection. He stirred in his seat, then rose, and with an uncertain step began to pace the room. His eye – heavy still, and filmy – caught mine.

'Ho! is that you?' he said in a peculiar voice, which scarcely seemed under the speaker's command. 'Hardly knew you were in the room – and Louisa too I declare! Well, I must have been adipose.[3] And what has Bromley said tonight? You were at chapel, somebody told me a while since – at least

7

I think so, but it may be all fancy! I daresay you'll think me in an extraordinary mood to-night, but I'll explain directly – as soon as I get sufficiently collected.'

With an unsteady hand he poured out a goblet of water, drank part, and, dipping his fingers in, cooled with the remainder his forehead and temples. 'My head throbs,' said he. 'I must not try this experiment often.' As he spoke, his hand shook so convulsively that he could hardly replace the glass on the table. Smiling grimly at this evidence of abused nerves, he continued,

'Really, Townshend! Only mark that! And what do you think it is occasioned by?'

'Intoxication,' I said concisely. 'And that of a very heathen kind. You were far better take to dry spirits at once, Macara, than do as you do.'

'Upon my conscience,' replied the Viscount, sitting down and striking the table with that same shaking hand. 'I do believe, Townshend, you are in the right. I begin to find that this system of mine, rational as I thought it, is fraught with the most irresistible temptation.'

Really, reader, it is difficult to deal with a man like Macara, who has candour at will to screen even his weakest points from attack. However infamous may be the position in which he is surprised, he turns round without a blush, and instead of defending himself, by denying that matters are as appearances would warrant you to suppose, usually admits all the disgrace of his situation, and begins with metaphysical profundity to detail all the motives and secret springs of action which brought matters to the state in which you found them.

According to this system of tactics the Viscount proceeded with his self-accusation.

'It was a fine evening, as you know,' said he, 'and I thought I would take a stroll up the valley, just to alleviate those low spirits which had been oppressing me all day. Townshend, I dare say you do not know what it is to look at an unclouded sun, at pleasant fields and young woods crowding green and bright to the edge of a river, and from these fair objects to be unable to derive any feeling but such as is tinged with sadness. However, I am familiar with this state of mind – and as I passed through the wicket that shuts in Louisa's lawn, and turning round paused in the green alley, and saw between the laurels the glittering red sky, clear as fire, which the sun had left far over the hills, I, Townshend, felt that, still and bright as the day was closing, fair as it promised to rise on the morrow, this summer loveliness was nothing to me – no.

'So I walked up to the house; I entered this room, wishing to find Louisa. She was not there, and when I inquired for her I was told she would not return for some hours. I sat down to wait. The dusk approached, and in that mood of mind I watched it slowly veiling every object, clothing every tree of the shrubbery, with such disguises as a haunted, a disturbed, a blackened imagination could suggest. Memory whispered to me that in former years I could have sat at such an hour, in such a scene; and from the rising moon, the darkening landscape on which I looked, the quiet little chamber where I sat, have gathered images all replete with bliss for the present, with softened happiness for the future. Was it so now? No, Mr Townshend; I was in a state of mind which I will not mock you by endeavouring to describe. But the gloom, the despair, became unendurable; dread forebodings rushed upon me, whose power I could not withstand. I felt myself on the brink of some hideous disaster and a vague influence ever and anon pushed me over, till clinging wildly to life and reason, I almost lost consciousness in the faintness of mortal terror.

'Now, Townshend, so suffering, how far did I err when I had resource to the sovereign specific which a simple narcotic drug offered me? I opened this little box, and, sir, I did not hesitate. No, I tasted. The change was wrought quickly. In five minutes I, who had been the most miserable wretch under that heaven, sat a rational, happy man, soothed to peace of mind, to rest of body, capable of creating sweet thoughts, of tasting bliss, of dropping those fetters of anguish which had restrained me, and floating away with light brain and soaring soul into the fairest regions imagination can disclose. Now, Townshend, I injured no fellow-creature by this: I did not even brutalize myself. Probably my life may be shortened by indulgence of this kind – but what of that? The eternal sleep will come sometime, and as well sooner as later.'

'I've no objection,' returned I, coolly. 'Louisa, have you?'

'I can't understand the pleasure of that opium,' said the Marchioness. 'And as to low spirits, I often tell Macara that I think there must be a great deal of fancy in them.'

The Viscount gently sighed, and, dropping his hand on hers, said, as he softly pressed it with his wan fingers, 'May you long think so, Louisa!'

Finding that his lordship was in much too sentimental a

mood to serve my turn, I shortly after rose and took my leave. The Marchioness attended me to the hall-door.

'Is he not *frénétique*, Charles?' said she. 'What nonsense to make such a piece of work about low spirits! I declare he reminds me of Ashworth. He, poor man, after a few days of hard preaching and harder drinking used to say that he had a muttering devil at his side. He told Bromley so once, and Bromley believed him. Would you have done, Charles?'

'Implicitly, madam. Goodnight.'

Charles Townshend decides to pay a visit to the country

I like the city. So long as winter lasts, it would be no easy task to entice me from its warm and crowded precincts. So long even as spring, with lingering chill, scatters her longer showers and fitful blinks of sunshine, I would cling to the theatre at night and the news-room[4] in the morning. But at last, I do confess, as June advances, and ushers in a long series of warm days, of soft sunsets and mellow moonlight evenings, I do begin to feel certain intuitive longings for an excursion, a jaunt out into the country, a sojourn somewhere far off, where there are woods, pastoral hills and bright pebbled becks.

This feeling came strong over me the other day, when, sitting in Grant's Coffee-House, I took up a fashionable paper whose columns teemed with such announcements as the following:

Preparations are making at Roslyn castle, the seat of Lord St Clair in the North, for the reception of his Lordship's family and a party of illustrious visitors, who are invited to spend the summer quarter amidst the beautiful forest scenery with which that part of the St Clair estate abounds.

Prince Augustus of Fidena set out yesterday, accompanied by his tutor, for Northwood-Zara, whither the Duke and Duchess of Fidena are to follow in a few days.

Lord and Lady Stuartville leave town to-morrow. Their destination is Stuartville Park in Angria.

The Earl of Northangerland is still at Selden House. It is understood that his lordship expresses little interest in politics.

General Thornton and his lady took their departure for Girnington Hall last week. The General intends adding to the plantations on his already finely wooded property in Angria.

The Earl and Countess of Arundel are at their seat of Summerfield House, in the province of Arundel.

General and Mrs Grenville propose to spend the summer at Warner Hall, the residence of W. H. Warner Esqre, premier of Angria.

John Bellingham Esqre, banker, is rusticating at Goldthorpe Mowbray. The physicians have advised sea bathing for the perfect restoration of Mr Bellingham's health, which has suffered considerably from a severe attack of influenza.

The Marquis of Harlaw, with a party of friends, J. Billinger Esqre, Mr Macqueen etc., is enjoying a brief relaxation from state cares at Colonel Luckyman's country house, Catton Lodge.

Lord Charles and the young ladies Flower have joined their noble mother at Mowbray. Sigston's Hotel is engaged entirely for the use of Lady Richton and her household. Lord Charles Flower, who, as well as his sisters, is just recovering from the measles, continues under the care of Dr Morrison, the family physician. The noble ambassador himself is in the south.

From these paragraphs it was evident that the season was now completely over. No more assemblies at Flower House, no more select dinner-parties at the Fidena Palace. Closed were the saloons of Thornton Hotel, forsaken were the squares round Ellrington Hall and Wellesley House, void were the habitations of Castlereagh, darkened the tabernacles of Arundel! Whereas now, in remote woods, the chimneys of Girnington Hall sent out their blue smoke to give token that the old spot was peopled again; in remoter meads, the broad sashes of Summerfield House were thrown up, to admit the gale sweeping over those wide prairies into rooms with mirrors cleared and carpets spread and couches unswathed in holland. Every blind was withdrawn at Stuartville Park, every shutter opened, and the windows through crimson curtains looked boldly towards the green ascent⁵ where Edwardston

13

smiles upon its young plantations. The rooks were cawing at Warner Hall with cheerier sound than ever as, early on a summer morning, the Prime Minister of Angria, standing on his front-door steps, looked at the sun rising over his still grounds and deep woods and over the long, dark moors of Howard.

I could have grown poetical. I could have recalled more distant and softer scenes touched with the light of other years, hallowed by higher – because older – associations than the campaign of –33, the rebellion of –36. I might have asked how sunrise yet became the elms and the turret of Wood Church. But I restrained myself, and merely put the question, shall I have me out or not? And whither shall I direct my steps? To my old quarters at the Greyhound opposite Mowbray Vicarage? To my friend Tom Ingham's farm at the foot of Boulshill? To some acquaintances I have North awa' in the vicinity of Fidena? Or to a snug country lodging I know of in the south not far from my friend Billinger's paternal home? Time and chance shall decide me. I've cash sufficient for the excursion; I've just rounded off my nineteenth year and entered on my twentieth; I'm a neat figure, a competent scholar, a popular author, a gentleman and a man of the world. Who then shall restrain me? Shall I not wander at my own sweet will? Allons, reader, come, and we will pack the carpet-bag. Make out an inventory: Item – 4 shirts, 6 fronts, 4 pair cotton, 2 pair silk stockings, 1 pair morocco pumps, 1 dress satin waistcoat, 1 dress coat, 2 pair dress pantaloons, 1 pair nankeens,[6] 1 brush and comb, 1 bottle macassar oil, 1 tooth-brush, box vegetable tooth-powder, 1 pot cream of roses, 1 case of razors (N.B. for show not use), two cakes of almond soap, 1 bottle eau de cologne, 1 bottle eau de mille fleurs, 1 pair curling-irons. C'est tout! I'm my own valet now! Reader, if you're ready, so am I. The coach is coming, hillo! Off at full speed to meet it!

At Stancliffe's Hotel, amongst the commercial travellers

'Well, I think I shall have to stay at Zamorna all night. It's a delightful June evening.' So I soliloquized to myself, as, standing in the traveller's room at Stancliffe's Hotel, I from the window watched the umbrellas, cloaks, and mackintoshes which ever and anon traversed Thornton Street in Zamorna. It had been market-day, and the gigs of the clothiers, now homeward-bound, were bowling along the pavement in the teeth of the driving showers and fitful blasts in which the before-mentioned delightful June evening had thought proper to veil its close. Now and then a cavalcade of some half-dozen mounted manufacturers passed the window at full trot. These gentlemen had doubtless dined *en comité* at the Woolpack or the Stuart Arms, and the speed and lightness of their progress, the pleasing gaiety of their aspects, and the frequency of the laugh and jest in their ranks indicated pretty plainly that they were, one and all – to speak technically – market-fresh.[7] Many of the gigs, too, shot past with a vengeable rapidity which warranted that [the] occupants had duly laid in the stock of brandy and water. Wild and boisterous as the wind swept up the street and drove before it a

15

heavy constant rain, these heroes, safe in the external shield of waterproof capes and the internal specific of no less waterproof cognac, dashed away towards the open Edwardston or Adrianopolitan roads, as if in defiance of the storm which was to meet them in fuller force when removed from the partial shelter of the city.

The traveller's room at Stancliffe's Hotel by no means exhibited the silence and solitude of a hermit's cell. Gentlemen in the soft and hard line strode in and out incessantly from the trampled inn-passage, whose wet and miry floor plainly told the condition of the streets outside. Then there were loud calls for the waiters, incessant ringings of the weary bell, orders about sundry carpet-bags and portmanteaus, deliveries of divers wet great-coats and drenched pea-surtouts[8] to be dried instantly at the kitchen-fire, expostulations about mysterious subjects unintelligible except to the affrighted waiter and the aggrieved complainant. One furious individual, whose gig drove up to the Hotel amidst the pelting of a wilder torrent of rain than had fallen in the course of the whole afternoon, entered the room with a dark and ominous aspect. As he was drawing off his three-caped great-coat, from which the water dripped in streams, something in the condition of the fire-place seemed to strike him with conscientious horror. He rushed to the door.

'Waiter! Waiter!! Waiter!!!' he exclaimed with the voice of a lion.

The waiter came. The person who had summoned him was a portly man and an apoplectic; his rage seemed at first to impede his utterance, but not for long. He opened forth:

'Look at that grate, sir! Do you call that comfort – tawdry rags of blue and yellow paper instead of a good fire?'

'It's June, sir,' replied the waiter. '18th inst. We never put on fire in the low-rooms after May goes out.'

'Damn you,' said the bagman. 'Light a fire directly, or I'll send for your master and give him a jobation[9] to his face about it. Let me tell you, your people here at Stancliffe's get abominably careless. Such a blackguard dinner as I had here last circuit! But I promise you if you set me down to such another I'll put up at the Stuart Arms in future. Light a fire, sir, and take my coat. If you leave a wet thread on it I'll subtract it from the reckoning. Bring me some hot punch and oysters for supper, and mind the chambermaid airs my bed well. I'd damp sheets last time I slept here, I'll be d—ed if I had not.'

Your Angrian commercial traveller is one of the greatest scamps in existence, much on a par with your Angrian newspaper editor. Anything more systematically unprincipled, more recklessly profligate than these men, taking them as a body, is not easy to conceive. Characters indicative of these vices were legibly written in the faces of the half-dozen gentlemen gathered on this stormy evening in the apartment to which I have introduced my readers. Conversation did not flag amongst them. Amidst the ringing of crushers and tumblers, such sentences were heard as the following:

'Brown, I say, you're lucky to have no further to go to-night!'

'Well, and so are you, an't you?'

'Me! I must push on ten miles further if it rain cats and dogs: I must be in Edwardston by nine to-night to meet one of our partners.'

'Which of them: Culpeper or Hoskins?'

'Culpeper, ac—d cross-grained dog.'

'Pretty weather, this, for June ain't it?' interpolated a young dandy with red curls and velvet waistcoat.

'Aye, as pretty as your phiz,' replied the furious man who had ordered the fire to be lit, and who was now sitting with both his feet on the fender, full in front of the few smoky coals which in obedience to his mandates had been piled together.

'I say, can you change me a bank-note?' asked one man with his chin shrouded in a white shawl.

'Bank of Angria or private bank?' said the person whom he had addressed.

'Private bank – of our own Amos Kirkwall and sons.'

'I can change it with our pound notes – Edward Percy's and Steaton's: I got them at their warehouse this afternoon.'

'I'd prefer these any day to sovereigns – less chance of their being counterfeit.'

'Well, and how go politics to-day?' asked a smart traveller in a gold chain, slapping on the shoulder a studious individual deeply absorbed in the perusal of a newspaper.

'God knows!' was the answer. 'I should not be much astonished to hear of the Prime Minister resigning.'

'And he will if he does his duty,' exclaimed a third person. 'Have you seen the *War Despatch* for this morning? My word, their people do go it!'

'Manly, independent print, the *War Despatch*,' answered the first speaker. 'Delivers the sentiments of the nation at large. Curse it – who's to hinder us from asserting our rights? Aren't we all free-born Angrians?'

'The *Rising Sun* swears that Percy has tendered his resignation, and been solicited to withdraw it. What do you think of that?'

'That he had a capital opportunity of discharging with interest many a long bill of insults he has been storing up against the Czar for these three years at least.'

'But I think it would hardly be like him to let such an opportunity pass, if it be so. Brandy and Water! He'll serve them out next sessions, in style.'

'By G—d, that he will, and *before* next sessions too. *A propos* of that, they say some of the leaders in the *War Despatch* are penned by him.'

'Very likely; he's a real trump-card. Do you deal with him?'

'No, our house is in the cutlery-line.'

'We do, or rather, we did a while since; but he screwed so hard in that last bargain about some casks of madder, and came down so prompt for payment at a time when ready money was rather scarce with us, that our senior partner swore upon the Gospels he'd burn his fingers in that oven no more.'

The furious man, who had hitherto sat silent, here turned from the fire which he had by this time coaxed into something like a blaze and growled sotto-voce: 'Shall be happy to supply you, Mr Drake, with madder, indigo, logwood and barilla of all qualities on the most reasonable terms. Shall feel obliged if you will favour me with an order. May I put you down?' He drew out a pocket-book and unsheathed a pencil.

'Of what house?' asked Mr Drake.

'I do for Milnes, Duff & Stephenson, Dyers, Anvale,' answered the fire-eater.[10]

'Humph!' rejoined Drake with a kind of sneer. 'I've seen that firm mentioned somewhere.' He affected to ponder for a moment, then, snapping his fingers: 'I have it! It was in the *Gazette*. Paid a second dividend, I think, a month ago – half-a-crown in the pound.'

The man of choler said nothing: he was flabbergasted. But he leaned back in his chair, and, lifting both feet from the fender, he deposited one on each hob. His favourite element, now burning clear and red, seemed to console him for every *contre-temps*.

'Drat it, the weather's clearing!' suddenly ejaculated that gentleman who had declared his obligation to be at Edwardston by nine o'clock. He rushed out of the room and, having peremptorily ordered his gig, rushed back again; and having swallowed the contents of a capacious tumbler besought Dawson to help him on with his d—d mackintosh. Then, as he settled the collar about his neck, he bade an affectionate adieu to the said Dawson in the words:

'Go it old cock! goodbye! Judging by thy nose next circuit will use thee up.'

I saw him from the window mount his gig and flash down the still wet street like a comet.

In truth, the clouds for the first time that day were now beginning to separate. The rain had cease[d]; the wind likewise had subsided; and I think, if I could have seen the west, the sun, within a few minutes of its setting, was just shedding one parting smile over the Olympian.[11] Several of the travellers now rose. There was a general ordering out of gigs and assuming of coats and cloaks. In a few minutes the room was cleared, with the exception of two or three whose intention it was to take up their quarters at Stancliffe's for the night. While these discussed professional subjects, I maintained my station at the window, watching the passengers whom the gleam of sunshine had called out at the close of a rainy day.

In particular, I marked the movements of a pretty woman who seemed waiting for someone at the door of a splendid mercer's shop opposite. Drawing aside the green blind, I tried to catch her eye, displaying a gold snuff-box under pretence of taking a pinch, and by the same action exhibiting two or three flashy rings with which my white aristocratic hand was adorned. Her eye was caught by the glitter. She looked at me from amongst a profusion of curls, glossy and silky though of the genuine Angrian hue.[12] From me her glance reverted to her own green silk frock and pretty sandalled feet. I fancied she smiled. Whether she did or not, I certainly returned the compliment by a most seductive grin. She blushed. Encouraged by this sign of sympathy, I kissed my hand to her. She giggled, and retreated into the shop. While I was vainly endeavouring to trace her figure, of which no more than the dim outline was visible through the gloom of the interior, increased by waving streamers of silk and print pendant to the shop door, someone touched my arm. I turned. It was a waiter.

'Sir, you are wanted, if you please.'

'Who wants me?'

'A gentleman upstairs. Came this afternoon. Dined here. I've just carried in the wine, and he desired me to tell the young gentleman in the traveller's room who wore a dark frock-coat and white jeans[13] that he would be happy to have the pleasure of his company for the evening.'

'Do you know who he is?' I asked.

'I've not heard his name, sir, but he came in his own carriage – a genteel barouche. A military looking person. I should fancy he may be an officer in the army.'

'Well,' said I, 'show me up to his apartment,' and as the slippered waiter glided before me I followed with some little curiosity to see who the owner of the genteel barouche might be. Not that there was anything at all strange in the circumstance, for Stancliffe's, being the head hotel in Zamorna, every day received aristocratic visitants within its walls. The Czar himself usually changed horses here in his journeys to and from his capital.

Charles Townshend remembers the trial of Zamorna, after his defeat at Edwardston, and meets an old friend

Traversing the inn-passage – wetter and dirtier than ever, and all in tumult for the evening Verdopolitan-coach had just come in and the passengers were calling for supper and beds and rooms and at the same time rushing wildly after their luggage – traversing, I say, this rich melée, in the course of which transit I nearly ran over a lady and a little girl and was in requital called a rude scoundrel by their companion, a big fellow in mustachios – traversing, I once more repeat, this area wherein a woman with a child in her arms – dripping wet, for she had ridden on the outside of the coach – came against me full drive, I at length, after turning the angle of [a] second long passage and passing through a pair of large folding doors, found myself in another region. It was a hall with rooms about it, green mats at every door, a lamp in the centre, a broad staircase ascending to a gallery above, which ran round three sides of the hall, leaving space in the fourth for a great arched window. All here was clean, quiet, stately. This was the new part of the hotel, which had been erected since the year of independence. Before that time, Stancliffe's was but a black-looking old public, whose best apartment was not more handsomely furnished than its present traveller's room. As I ascended the staircase, chancing to look through the window I got a full and noble view of that new court-house which, rising upon its solid basement, so majestically fronts the first inn in Zamorna. There it was that, after the disastrous day of Edwardston, Jeremiah Simpson opened his court martial; there, on such an evening as this. At this very hour, when twilight was sealing sunset, a turbaned figure, with furred robes like a sultan and shawl streaming from his waist, had mounted those steps, and, while all the wide and long street beneath him was a sea of heads and a hell of strange cries, had shouted: 'Soldiers, bring on the prisoner!' Then, breaking through the crowd, trampling down young and old, Julian Gordon's troopers burst on amidst the boom of Quashia's gongs and the yell of Medina's kettle-drums. A gun mounted on the court-house was discharged down on the heads of the mob, as was afterwards sworn before the House of Peers. Through the smoke the prisoner could hardly be seen, but his head was bare, his hands bound; that court-house received him, and the door was barred on the mob.

'This is the room, sir,' said the waiter, throwing open a door in the middle of the gallery, and admitting me to a large apartment whose style of decoration, had I been a novice in such matters, would have burst upon me with dazzling force. It was as elegant in finish, as splendid in effect, as a saloon in any nobleman's house. The windows were large, lofty and clear; the curtains were of silk that draperied them, of crimson silk, imparting to everything a rosy hue. The carpet was soft and rich, exhibiting groups of brilliant flowers. The mantelpiece was crowned with classical ornaments – small but exquisite figures in marble, vases as white as snow, protected from soil by glass bells inverted over them, silver lamps, and, in the centre, a foreign time-piece. Above all these sloped a picture, the only one in the room: an Angrian peer in his robes, really a fine fellow. At first I did not recognize the face, as the costume was so unusual; but by degrees I acknowledged a dashing likeness to the most noble Frederick Stuart, Earl of Stuartville and Viscount Castlereagh, Lord Lieutenant of the Province of Zamorna. 'Really,' thought I, as I took in the *tout ensemble* of the room, 'These Angrians do lavish the blunt – hotels like palaces, palaces like Genii dreams.[14] It's to be hoped there's cash to answer the paper-money, that's all.' At a table covered with decanters and silver fruit-baskets sat my unknown friend, the owner of the genteel conveyance.

The waiter having retired, closing the door after him, I advanced.

William Percy tells Charles Townshend of his exploits

It being somewhat dusk, and the gentleman's face being turned away from the glow of a ruddy fire, I did not at first glance hit his identity. However, I said,

'How do you do, sir? Glad to see you.'

'Pretty well, thank you,' returned he, and slowly rising, he tenderly took his coat-tails under the protection of his arms, and standing on the rug presented his back to the before-mentioned ruddy fire.

'O it's you, is it!' I ejaculated; for his face was now obvious enough. 'How the devil did you know that I was here?'

'What the d—l brought you here?' he asked.

'Why the devil do you wish to know?' I rejoined.

'How the devil can I tell?' he replied.

Here, our wits being mutually exhausted by these brilliant sallies, I took a momentary reprieve in laughter. Then my friend began again.

'In God's name, take a chair.'

'In Christ's name, I will.'

'For the love of Heaven, let me fill you a bumper.'

'For the fear of Hell, leave no heel-tap.'[15]

'I adjure you by the gospels, tell me if it's good wine.'

'I swear upon the Koran, I've tasted better.'

'By the miracle of Cana, you lie.'

25

'By the miracle of Moses, I do not.'

'According to your oaths, sir, I should take you to be circumcised.'

'According to yours, I should scarce think you were baptized.'

'The Christian ordinance came not upon me.'

'The Mahometan rite I have eschewed.'

'Thou then art an unchristened Heathen.'

'And thou an infidel Giaour.'[16]

'Pass the bottle, lad,' said my friend, resuming his seat and grasping the decanter with emphasis. He and I filled our glasses, and then we looked at each other. A third person, I think, would have observed something similar about us. We were both young, both thin, both sallow and light-haired and blue-eyed, both carefully and somewhat foppishly dressed, with small feet set off by a slender *chaussure* and white hands garnished with massive rings. My friend, however, was considerably taller than I, and had besides more of the air military. His head was differently set upon his shoulders. He had incipient light brown mustaches and some growth of whisker; he threw out his chest too and sported a length of limb terminating in boot and spur. His complexion, originally fair almost to delicacy, appeared to have seen service, for it was like my own much tan[ned], freckled and yellowed to a bilious hue with the sun. He wore a blue dress-coat with velvet collar, velvet waistcoat and charming white tights: I endued[17] a well-made green frock and light summer jeans. Now, reader, have you got us before you?

The young officer, resting his temples on his hand and

pensively filling a tall champagne glass, renewed the conversation.

'You'll be surprised to see me here, I daresay, aren't you?'

'Why yes; I thought you were at Gazemba or Dongola, or Bonowen or Socatoo, or some such barbarian station, setting slot-hounds on Negro-tracks, and sleeping like Moses among the flags on some river-side.'

'Well, Townshend,' said he. 'Your description exactly answers to the sort of life I have led for the last six months.'

'And are you stalled of it?' I asked.

'Stalled, man! think of the honour! Have you not seen in every newspaper: "The exertions of the 10th Hussars in the east under their Colonel Sir William Percy continue unabated. The efforts made by that Gallant Officer to extirpate the savages are beyond all praise. Scarce a day passes but five or six are hung under the walls of Dongola"? Then again: "A signal instance of vengeance was exhibited at Katagoom last week, by order of Sir William Percy. A soldier had been missing some days from his regiment stationed at that place. His remains were at length found in a neighbouring jungle, hideously mangled, and displaying all the frightful mutilation of Negro slaughter. Sir William instantly ordered out two of the fiercest and keenest hounds in his leashes. They tracked up the murderers in a few hours. When seized, the blood-stained wretches were sunk up to the neck in the deep mire of a carr-brake.[18] Sir William had them shot through the head where they stood, and their bodies merged in the filth which afforded them such a suitable sepulchre." Eh, Townshend? is not that the strain?'

'Exactly so. But now Colonel, since you were so honour-ably occupied, why do I now find you so far from the seat of your glorious toil?'

'Really, Townshend, how can you be so unreasonable? The tenth Hussars – all Gods as they are, or God-like men, which is better – can't stand the sun of those deserts and the malaria of those marshes for ever. It has therefore pleased our gracious monarch to command a recall; that is, not by his own sacred mouth, but through the medium of W. H. Warner Esqre, our trusty and well-beloved councillor, who delivered his instructions to our General-in-Chief and Commander of the Forts, Henri Fernando di Enara, by whom they were transmitted to your humble servant.'

'And with alacrity you jumped at the reprieve.'

'Jumped at it? No; I perused the despatch with, I believe, my wonted coolness – awed, of course, by the sublime appel-lation of our Lord the King, in whose name it was penned – but otherwise I sweat not, neither did I swoon. It is not for us poor subalterns to feel either joy or grief, satisfaction or disappointment.'

'Well, Colonel, where are you going now?'

'Lord, Mr Townshend, don't be in such a hurry! Let one have a minute's time for reflection! I've hardly yet got over the anguish of soul that came upon me at Gazemba.'

'How? On what account?'

'All a sense of my own insignificance – a humbling to the dust, as it were. That organ of veneration is so predominant in my cranium, it will be the death of me some day. You know, being to go to Adrianopolis, it was needful to pass through Gazemba, and being at Gazemba, it was onerous to wait upon our Commander of the Forts at his pretty little villa there. So, having donned the regimentals over a check shirt for the more grace (it would have been presumptuous to appear in cambric while his Highness sported huckaback), I made my way to the domicile. Signor Fernando must be a man of some nerves to endure about his person such fellows as form the household of that garrison. The dirtiest dregs of a convict hulk would scarce turn out such another muster. Parricides, matricides, fratricides, sororicides, stabbers in the dark, blackguard bullies of hells,[19] scoundrel suborners of false testimony: of these materials has he formed the domestic establishment of his country-seat. A forger in the disguise of a porter opened the door for me; a cut-purse wearing a foot-man's epaulettes shewed me to an ante-room; there I was received by one bearing a steward's wand who had been thrice convicted of arson; he gave my name to a Mr Secretary Gordon, who had visibly been hanged for murder but unfortunately cut down before the law had done its perfect work.

'Of course I sweat[ed] profusely by the time I had passed through this ordeal, and when at length Mr Gordon introduced me to a dismal little dungeon called a cabinet where sat Enara, my knees shook under me like aspen leaves. There was the great man in his usual attire of a gingham jacket and canvas trousers of more than Dutch capacity. Stock[20] he disdained, and waistcoat: the most fastidious lady might have beheld with admiration that muscular chest and neck bristled with heroic hair. Between the commander's lips breathed a cigar, and in one hand he held a smart box of the commodity,

29

fresh as imported from the spicy islands where springs the fragrant weed. With head a little declined, and brow contracted in solicitude respecting the important choice, the illustrious General seemed, at the moment I entered, to be engaged in picking out another of the same. Mark the noble simplicity of a great mind stooping to the commonest employment of an ordinary shop-boy! Having made his election, he handed the Havannah to a person who stood beside him, and whom till now I had not perceived, ejaculating as he did so, "Damn it! I think that'll be a good 'un!" "G—d, so it is!" was his companion's answer when, after a moment's pause, he had tried the sweet Virginian. I looked now at this second speaker. Townshend, it was too much! At Enara's chair back there stood a man in a shabby brown surtout, with his hands stuck in the hind pockets thereof, wearing a stiff stock, out of which projected a long and dark dried vinegar physiognomy shaded with grizzly whiskers and overshaded with still more grizzly hair. The fellow was so ugly, at first sight I thought it must be a stranger. A second glance assured me that it was General Lord Hartford. What could I do? The blaze of patrician dignity quite overpowered me. However, I made shift to advance.

"'How d'ye do, Sir William?" said Enara. "Recalled, you find? I regret the necessity, which doubtless will be a great disappointment to you." I ventured to ask in what respect? He looked at me as if I had put the question in Greek. "As a man of honour, sir, I should suppose – but most probably you are consoling yourself under the disappointment by the prospect of a speedy return. We shall see, sir; I will speak to the Duke in your behalf. Your services have given me much satisfaction." I bowed, of course, and then stood to hear what more was coming, but the General seemed to have said his say. Lord Hartford now grunted something unintelligible, though with the most dignified air possible, his underlip being scornfully protruded to support the cigar and his branded brow corrugated over his eyes with the sour malignant look of a fiend. He seemed to breathe asthmatically, I suppose in consequence of that wound he received last winter. Finding that there was no more talk to be had for love or money, I rose to go. In reply to my farewell genuflection Enara nodded sharply, and muttered a word or two about hoping to see me again soon and having a spot of special work cut out purposely for me. Hartford bent his stiff back with a stern haughty bow that made me feel strongly inclined to walk round behind him and trip up his heels.'

I laughed as Sir William closed his narration.

'Well, you do give it them properly, Colonel!' said I. 'A set of pompous prigs! I like to hear them dished now and then. And how did you get on at Adrianopolis? I suppose you saw the premier?'

'Yes, I went to the Treasury; and I'd scarcely got within the door of his parlour there before he began in his woman's voice, "Sir William, Sir William, let me hear what you have been doing. Give a clear account, sir, of your proceedings. General Enara's despatches are not sufficiently detailed, sir; they are too brief, too laconic. The government of the country is kept in the dark, sir – comparatively speaking that is – at a time, too, when every facility for obtaining information ought to be afforded it. I wish to know every particular concerning that late affair at Cuttal-Curafee." He stopped a minute, and looked at me. I looked at him, and sat down, after settling the cushion on my chair. The pause being a rather lengthened one, I remarked that it was a fine morning. "What?" said he, pricking up his ears. "The morning is charmingly cool and dry," was my answer. "Is it possible?" exclaimed Warner. "Sir, I say, is it possible that the trite remarks of the most indolent and vacant time-killer should be the first and only words on the lips of a man just returned from the active service of his king, in a country reeking with rapine and carnage and teeming with the hideous pollutions of pagan savages?" "What do you wish me to say?" I asked, taking up a pamphlet that lay on the table and glancing at the title-page. "Sir," said the premier, very lofty and impressive. "Sir, my time is valuable. If your business with me is not of so important a nature as to require immediate attention we will defer it for the present." Endeavouring to suppress a yawn, and slightly stretching my limbs – not inelegant, are they Townshend? – I replied: "Business, sir? Your honour, I hardly know what I called upon you for. It was merely, I think, to pass away an idle hour. Can you tell me what the newest fashions are? I'm quite out just now in dress, for really one sees little in that line at Cuttal-Curafee." "Sir," replied Warner, "I wish you a very good morning. Mr Jones will show you the door." "Good morning, sir," said I, and I left the Treasury as good as kicked out.'

'Well, and where did you go next?'

'I went to a perfumers, and bought a few trifles in the

way of gloves and combs. On returning, whom do you think I met?'

'Can't guess.'

'Why, none other than the President to the Board of Trade.'

'What! Edward Percy?'

'Yes; he stopt in the street and began: "William! I say, William, who sent for you back? I know it for a fact, sir, that you sent up a puling memorial soliciting a recall. You did, sir, don't begin to deny it."

'"Not [I]," I answered. "Good morning, Edward! Charming seasonable weather! Take care of your lungs, lad – always pthisically inclined. I would recommend balsam of horehound – excellent remedy for pulmonary complaints! Good morning, lad!" And gracefully waving my hand, I passed on.'

Here a waiter came in with wax-lights and a supper-tray. Sir William invited me to partake of his roast chicken and oyster-sauce, but I declined, as I had ordered supper on my own account in a room below. We separated therefore for the night, after shaking hands in the Colonel's peculiar way – that is, a cool presentation of each individual's fore-finger.

Charles Townshend and Sir William Percy engage in a flirtation

The next morning rose as lovely and calm a day as ever ushered in the steps of summer. Wakened by the sunshine – I saw it streaming in through the stately windows of my

33

chamber between the interstices of the carefully drawn curtains – my heart was rejoiced at the sight, and still more so when, on rising and withdrawing that veil, I beheld, in the lofty and dappled arch of a few marbled clouds, in the serenity and freshness of the air, a soft promise of settled summer. The storms, the fitful showers and chilly gusts, to which for the last month we had been subject, were all gone. They had swept the sky and left it placid behind them.

It took me a full half hour to dress, and another half hour to view myself over from head to foot in the splendid full-length mirror with which my chamber was furnished. Really, when I saw the neat figure therein reflected, genteelly attired in a fashionable morning suit, with light soft hair parted on one side and brushed into glossy curls, I thought, 'there are worse men in the world than Charles Townshend'. Having descended from my chamber, I made my way once again into the bustling, dirty inn-passage before described. It was bustling still, but not so dirty as it had been the night before, for a scullion wench was on her knees with a huge pail, scouring away for the bare life. A gentleman's carriage was at the door. Two or three servants were lifting into it some luggage, and a family party stood waiting to enter – a lady, a gentleman, and some children. The children, indeed, were already mounted behind, and a stout rosy Angrian brood they looked. Their mother was receiving the parting civilities of a fine, tall, showy woman, most superbly dressed, who had come sailing out of a side room to see them off. It was Mrs Stancliffe, the hostess of this great house. I went up to her when the carriage had at length driven away, and paid my respects, for I had some little significance with her. She received and answered my attentions much in the tone and with the air of the Countess of Northangerland, only more civilly. Let not the Countess hear me, but it is a fact that she and the landlady bear a strong resemblance to each other, being nearly equal in point of longitude, latitude and circumference. Big women both! awful women! In temper, too, they are somewhat like, as the following anecdote will shew.

A public dinner being given a few months since by the Corporation of Zamorna to their Lord Lieutenant, the Earl of Stuartville, and to Sir Wilson Thornton, in honour of the eminent services rendered by those officers to their country in the war campaign, the whole conduct of culinary matters was of course consigned to the superintendence of Mrs Stancliffe. It so happened that, by some oversight or other, the individual with whom she had contracted for a supply of game failed in his duty. On the great day of the feast, the tables were spread in the court-house. Stancliffe's plate, conveyed over the way in iron chests, shone in tasteful arrangement and more than princely splendour on the ample boards. The gentlemen of the province were collected from far and near. The hour of six struck; the soup and fish were on the table.

The Lord Lieutenant walked in amidst deafening cheers, looking as much the fine gentleman as ever, and smiling and bowing his thanks to his townsmen. General Sir William Thornton followed and Edward Percy Esqre, M.P. Last, though not least, the proud, bitter owner of Hartford Hall entered, with a face like an unbleached holland sheet (it was after his wound), supported between Sir John Kirkwall and

Wm Moore Esqre, an eminent barrister. A blessing being solemnly pronounced by the Right Reverend Dr Kirkwall, primate of Zamorna, and Amen responded by Dr Cook, vicar of Edwardston, all fell to. Fish and soup being despatched, game ought to have entered. But instead of it, in walked Mrs Stancliffe, grandly dressed, with a turban and a plume and a diamond aigrette[21] like any countess in the gallery. She went to the back of Lord Stuartville's chair.

'My lord,' said she, with great dignity of manner and in a voice sufficiently audible to be heard by everyone present. 'I ought to apologize to your lordship for the delay of the second course, but my servants have failed in their duty and it is not forthcoming. However, I have punished the insult thus offered to your lordship and the gentlemen of Zamorna. I have revolutionized my houshold. Before to-morrow night, not an ostler or a chambermaid of the present set shall remain in my employment.'

The bland Earl, passing his hand over his face to conceal a smile, said something gallant and polite by way of consolation to the indignant lady, and General Thornton assured her that such was the luxurious profusion and exquisite quality of her other provisions, two or three hares and partridges would never be missed. Mrs Stancliffe, however, refused to be comforted. Without at all relaxing the solemn concern of her countenance, she dropped a stately curtsey to the company and sailed away. She did revolutionize her household, and a pretty revolution it was, never such a helter-skelter turn out of waiters, barmaids, ostlers, boots and coachmen seen in this world before. Ever since this imperial move she has been popularly termed the Duchess of Zamorna! So Lord Stuartville delights to call her, even to her face. This is a liberty, however, taken by none but his gallant lordship. If any other man were to venture so far she'd soon spurt out in his face.

I had scarcely finished my breakfast when a waiter brought me a billet to the following effect: 'Dear Townshend, will you take a walk with me this morning? yours etc. W. Percy'. I scribbled for answer: 'Dear Baronet, with all the xcing. Yours etc. C. Townshend'. We met each other in the passage; and arm in arm, each with a light cane in his hand, started on our jaunt.

Zamorna was all astir. Half her population seemed poured out into the wide new streets. Not a trace remained of last night's storm. Summer was reigning with ardour in the perfectly still air and unclouded sunshine. Ladies in white dresses flitted along the streets and crowded the magnificent and busy shops. Before us rose the new minster, lifting its beautiful front and rich fretted pinnacles almost as radiant as marble against a sky of southern purity. Its bells, sweet-toned as Bochea's harp, rang out the morning chimes high in air, and young Zamorna seemed wakened to quicker life by the voice of that lofty music. How had the city so soon sprung to perfect vigour and beauty from the iron crush of Simpson's hoof? Here was no mark of recent tyranny, no trace of grinding exaction, no symptom of a lately repulsed invasion, of a now existing heavy national debt, nothing of squalor or want or suffering. Lovely women, stately mansions, busy mills and gorgeous shops appeared on all sides. When we first came out the atmosphere was quite clear. As we left the west end and approached the bridge and river, whose banks were piled with enormous manufactories and bristled with mill-chimneys, tall, stately, and steep as slender towers, we breathed a denser air. Columns of smoke as black as soot rose thick and solid from the chimneys of two vast erections – Edward Percy's, I believe, and Mr Sydenham's – and, slowly spreading, darkened the sky above all Zamorna.

'That's Edward's tobacco-pipe,' said Sir William, looking up, as we passed close under his brother's mill-chimney, whose cylindrical pillar rose three hundred feet into the air. Having crossed the bridge, we turned into the noble road which leads down to Hartford, and now the full splendour of the June morning began to disclose itself round us.

Immediately before us, the valley of the Olympian opened broad and free; the road with gentle descent wound white as milk down among the rich pastures and waving woods of the vale. My heart expanded as I looked at the path we were to tread, edging the feet of the gentle hills whose long sweep subsided to level on the banks of the river – the glorious river! brightly flowing, in broad quiet waves and with a sound of remote seas, through scenery as green as Eden. We were almost at the gates of Hartford Park. The house was visible far away among its sunny grounds, and its beech-woods, extending to the road, lifted high above the causeway a silver shade. This was not a scene of solitude. Carriages smoothly rolled past us every five minutes, and stately cavaliers galloped by on their noble chargers.

We had walked on for a quarter of an hour, almost in silence, when Sir William suddenly exclaimed,

'Townshend, what a pretty girl!'

'Where?' I asked.

He pointed to a figure a little in advance of us: a young lady, mounted on a spirited little pony, and followed by a servant, also mounted. I quickened my pace to get a nearer view. She wore a purple habit, long and sweeping; it disclosed a fine, erect and rounded form, set off to advantage by the grace of her attitude and the ease of all her movements. When I first looked, her face was turned away, and concealed partly by the long curls of her hair and partly by her streaming veil, but she presently changed her position, and then I saw a fine decided profile, a bright eye, and a complexion of exquisite bloom. From the first moment I knew she was not a stranger.

'I've seen that face before,' said I to Sir William. Then, as my recollection cleared, I added, 'It was last night in the mercer's shop opposite Stancliffe's.' For in fact this was the very girl whom I had watched from the window.

'I, too, have seen her before,' returned the Baronet. 'I know her name. It is Miss Moore, the daughter of the noted barrister.'

'What!' I exclaimed. 'Jane – the beautiful Angrian?' Perhaps my readers may recollect a description of this young lady which appeared some time since, in a sort of comparison between Eastern and Western women.

Sir William proceeded. 'I saw her last autumn at the musical festival which was held in September in the minster at Zamorna. You remember the anecdote concerning her which was told in the papers at that time?'

'Can't say I do.'

'Why, people said that she had particularly attracted the attention of His Majesty, who attended the Festival, and that he has bestowed on her the title of the Rose of Zamorna.'

'Was it true?'

'No further than this: she sat full in his sight and he stared at her as everybody else did, for she really was a very imposing figure in her white satin dress and stately plume of snowy ostrich feathers. He asked her name, too, and when somebody told him, he said, "By God, she's the Rose of Zamorna! I don't see another woman to come near her." That was all. I daresay he never thought of her afterwards. She's not one of his sort.'

'Well, but,' continued I, 'I should like to see a little more of her. Heigho! I believe I'm in love!'

'So am I,' said Percy, echoing the sigh. 'Head over ears! Look now, did you ever see a better horse-woman? What grace and spirit! But there's that cursed angle in the road, it will hide her. There, she's turned it. I declare, my sun is eclipsed. Is not yours, Townshend?'

'Yes, totally; but can't we follow her, Colonel? Where does she live?'

'Not far off. I really think we might manage it, though I never was introduced to her in my life, nor you either, I dare say.'

'To my sorrow, never.'

'Well then, have you any superfluous modesty? Because if you have, put it into your waistcoat pocket and button your coat over it. Now, man, are you eased of the commodity?'

'Perfectly.'

'Come along, then. Her father is a barrister and attending the assizes at Angria. Consequently, he is not at home. What so natural as for two elegant young men like you and I to be wanting him on business, respecting a mortgage – on a friend's estate, possibly, or probably on our own – or a lawsuit concerning our rich old uncle's contested will? The servants having answered that Mr Moore is not at home, can't we inquire for his daughter (she has no mother by the bye), to give her some particular charge which we won't entrust to menials? Now, man, have you got your cue?'

I put my thumb to the side of my nose, and we mutually strode on.

Mr Moore's house is a lease-hold on Lord Hartford's property, and he has the character in Zamorna of being a toady of that nobleman's. The barrister, though an able man, is certainly, according to report, but lightly burdened with principle, and it is possible that with his large fortune he may have hopes of one day contesting the election of the city with its present representative – in which case Lord Hartford's influence would be no feather in the scale of success.

'We enter here,' said Percy, pausing at a green gate which opened sweetly beneath an arch of laburnums upon a lawn like velvet. A white-walled villa stood before us, bosomed in a blooming shrubbery, with green walks between the rose-trees and a broad carriage-road winding through all to the door. In that bright hour (it was now nearly noon) nothing could be more soothing than its aspect of shade and retirement. One almost preferred it to the wide demesne and princely mansion which it fronted with such modest dignity. Arrived at the door, Sir William knocked. A footman opened it.

'Is Mr Moore within?'

'No, sir; master left home last week for the assizes.'

Sir William affected disappointment. He turned, and made a show of consulting me in a whisper. Then again, addressing the servant:

'Miss Moore is at home, perhaps?'

'Yes, sir.'

'Then be kind enough to give in our names to her – Messrs Clarke and Gardiner – and say we wish to see her for an instant on a matter of some importance.'

The servant bowed, and politely requesting us to walk forward, threw open the door of a small sitting-room.

The apartment was prettily furnished. Its single large window, flung wide open, admitted the faint gale which now and then breathed over the languor of the burning noon. This window looked specially pleasant, for it had a deep recess and a seat pillowed with a white cushion, over which waved the festoons of a muslin curtain. Seating ourselves within this embayment,[22] we leaned over the sill, and scented the jessamine whose tendrils were playing in the breeze around the casement.

'This is Miss Moore's own parlour,' said Sir William pointing to a little work-table with scissors, thimble and lace upon it, and then reverting his eye to a cabinet piano with an open music book above its key-board. 'I always appropriate when I'm left alone in a lady's boudoir,' he continued; and getting up softly, he was on the point of prigging[23] something from the work-table, when a voice slightly hummed in the passage, and without any other sound, either of footstep or rustling dress, Miss Moore like an apparition dawned upon us. The Colonel turned, and she was there. He looked at her, or rather through her, before he spoke. Really, she seemed to be haloed – there was something so radiant in her whole appearance. Not the large dark eyes of the west, nor the large even arch of the eye-brow; not the enthusiastic and poetic look, nor the braided or waving locks of solemn shade; but just a girl in white, plump and very tall. Her riding-habit was gone, and her beaver; and golden locks (the word golden I use in courtesy, mind, reader) drooped on the whitest neck in Angria. Her complexion seemed to glow: it was so fair, so blooming. She had very rosy lips and a row of small even teeth sparkling like pearls; her nose was prominent and straight and her eyes very spirited. Regularity of feature by no means formed her chief charm: it was the perfection of a lively complexion and handsome figure.

The lady looked very grave; her curtsey was dignified and distant.

'Permit me, madam,' said the Colonel, 'to introduce myself and my friend. I am Mr Clarke, this gentleman, Mr Gardiner. We are both clients of your father. You will have heard him mention the lawsuit now pending between Clarke and Gardiner versus Jowett.'

'I daresay,' returned Miss Moore, 'though I don't recollect just now. Will you be seated, gentlemen?'

She took her own seat on a little couch near the work-table and, resting her elbow on the arm, looked very graceful and majestic.

'A warm morning,' observed Sir William, by way of keeping up the conversation.

'Very,' she replied demurely.

'A pretty place Mr Moore has here,' said I.

'Rather,' was Miss Moore's answer; then, carelessly taking up her work, she continued. 'How can I serve you, gentlemen?'

Sir William rubbed his hand. He was obliged to recur to business.

'Why, madam, will you be so good as to say to Mr Moore when he returns that James Cartwright, the witness who was so reluctant to come up, has at length consented to appear, and that consequently the trial may proceed, if he thinks proper, next month.'

'Very well,' said she. Then, still bending her eyes upon the lace, she continued. 'How far have you come to tell my father this? Do you reside in the neighbourhood?'

'No, madam, but we are both on a visit there at present. We came to look after some little mill-property we possess in Zamorna.'

'You must have had a hot walk,' pursued Miss Moore. 'Will you take some refreshment?'

We both declined, but she took no notice of our refusal, and, touching a bell, ordered the servant who answered it to bring wine etc. She then quietly returned to her lace-work. We might have been lap-dogs or children for all the discomposure our presence seemed to occasion her. Sir William was a match for her, however. He sat, one leg crossed over the other, regarding her with a hard stare. I believe she knew his eyes were fixed upon her, but she kept her countenance admirably. At last he said,

'I have had the pleasure of seeing you before, madam.'

'Probably, sir; I don't always stay at home.'

'It was in Zamorna Minster last September.'

She did colour a little, and laughed, for she recollected, doubtless, the admiration with which her name had been mentioned at that time in the journals, and the thousand eyes which had been fixed upon her as the centre of attraction as she sat in her white satin robe high placed in the lofty gallery of the minster.

'A great many people saw me at that time,' she answered, 'and talked about me too, for my size gave me wonderful distinction.'

'Nothing but size?' asked Sir William, and his look expressed the rest.

'Will you take some salmagundi,[24] Mr Clarke?' said she, rising and approaching the tray which the servant had just placed on the table. Mr Clarke expressed his willingness; so did Mr Gardiner. She helped both, plentifully, and they fell to.

A knock came to the door. She stept to the window and looked out. I saw her nod and smile, and her smile was by no means a simper: it showed her front teeth, and made her eyes shine very pleasantly. She walked into the passage, and opened the door herself.

'Now, Jane, how are you?' said a masculine voice. Percy winked at me.

'How are you?' she answered. 'And why are you come here this hot day?'

'What! you're not glad to see me, I guess,' returned the visitor.

'Yes I am, because you look so cool! I'm sorry we've no fire to warm you, but you can step into the kitchen.'

'Come, be steady! Moore's at Angria, varry like?'

'Varry like he is – but you may walk forwards notwithstanding.' Then, in a lower voice, 'I've two chits in my parlour – very like counting-house clerks or young surgeons or something of that kind. Just come and look at them.'

Percy and I arrested the victual on the way to our mouths. We were wroth.

'The jade!' said Percy.

I said nothing. However, a more urgent cause of disturbance was at hand. That voice which had been speaking sounded but too familiar, both to Sir William and myself, and now the speaker was approaching with measured step and the clank of a spur. He continued talking as he came:

'I've come to dine with you, Jane, and then I've to step over to Hartford Hall about some business. I'll call again at six o'clock, and Julia says you've to come back with me to Girnington.'

'Whether I will or not, I suppose, General?'

'Whether you will or not.'

And here Sir Wilson Thornton paused, for he was in the room, and his glance had encountered us, seated at the table and tucking in[to] the wines with which Miss Moore had provided us. I don't think either Sir William or I changed countenance. General Thornton's eye always assumes a cold annoyed expression when it sees me. I met him freely:

46

'Ho! General! how d'ye do? My word, you do look warm with walking! Is your face swelled?'

'Not 'at I know on, Mr Townshend,' he answered coldly, and, bowing to Sir William, he took his seat.

'My dear General,' I continued. 'Don't on any account drink water in your present state. You seem to me to be running thin! I wish you may not catch your death of cold! Dear, dear – what a pity you should appear such a figure before a beautiful young lady like Miss Moore!'

'If I'm any vex to Miss Moore she'll be good enough to tell me of it without yer interference,' said the General, much disturbed.

'Had you ever the scarlet fever?' I inquired anxiously.

'I cannot see how my health concerns you,' he answered.

'Or the sweating sickness?' I continued.

The General brushed the dust from his coat-sleeve and, turning briskly to Miss Moore, asked her if these were the lads she had taken for two young surgeons.

'Yes,' said she, 'but I begin to think I was in the wrong.'

'I would like to know what nonsense brought 'em here,' said Thornton. 'They're no more surgeons nor I am. Percy, I wonder ye'll go looking abâat t' country wi' such a nout as Townshend.'

'Percy!' exclaimed Miss Moore. 'O, it is Sir William Percy! I thought I had seen that gentleman before. It was at a review: he was one of the royal staff.'

The Colonel bowed. 'The greatest compliment I ever had paid me,' said he, 'that Miss Moore should single me out from among thousands and recollect my face.'

'Just because it struck me for its likeness to Lord North-angerland's,' replied she.

'From whatever cause, madam, the honour is mine, and I am proud of it.'

He searched her countenance with one of those sentimental and sinister glances which, when they flicker in his eyes, do indeed make him strongly resemble his father. I don't think he was pleased with the result of his scrutiny. Miss Moore's aspect remained laughing and open as ever. Had she blushed or shrunk away, Sir William would have triumphed. But hers was no heart to be smitten with sudden, secret and cankering love – the sort of love he often aims to inspire.

'Come, Townshend,' said he, drawing on his gloves. 'We will go.'

'I think you'd better, lad,' observed Thornton. 'Neither you nor Townshend have done yourselves any credit by this spree.'

We both were bold enough to approach Miss Moore; and she was good-natured or thoughtless enough to shake hands with us freely, and say that when her father came home she should be happy to see his clients Messrs Clarke and Gardiner again, either about the lawsuit or to take a friendly cup of tea with them. The girl, to do her justice, seemed to have some tact. I don't think I shall soon forget her very handsome face, or the sound of her voice and the pleasant expression of her eyes.

As we two passed again through the embowered gate and stept out into the now burning road, I asked Sir William if he was smitten.

'Not I,' said he. 'There's no mind there, and very little

heart. If ever I marry, rest satisfied my choice will not fall upon the Rose of Zamorna.'

Yet something had evidently gone wrong with the young Colonel. His vanity was wounded, or he was vexed at the interference of General Thornton. Whatever the cause was, certain it [is] he grew mightily disagreeable, snapping on all sides and snarling sourly at everything. We had not walked above a quarter of a mile, when he said he had business which called him elsewhere, and he must now bid me good-day. The Baronet turned into a retired lane branching from the main road, and I continued my course straight on.

Jane Moore, staying at Girnington with General and Lady Thornton, sings stirring songs of the charge of the men of Ardsley and of the siege of Evesham in the recent Angrian war. Castlereagh, Earl of Stuartville, brings news that Zamorna is expected in Zamorna City next day, and that the populace, who are furious that he has been visiting Northangerland, are threatening to riot

The rumour of invaders through all Zamorna ran.
Then Turner Grey his watch-word gave:
        Ho! Ardsley to the van!

Lord Hartford called his yeomen, and Warner raised his clan,
But first in fiercest gallop rushed Ardsley to the van!
On came Medina's turbans, Sir John hurled his ban:
'Mid the thousand hearts who scorned it still Ardsley kept the van!

49

The freshening gales of battle a hundred standards fan,
And doubt not Ardsley's pennon floats foremost in the van!
Cold on the field of carnage they have fallen man for man,
And no more in march or onslaught will Ardsley lead the van!

Loud wail lamenting trumpets for all that gallant clan,
And Angrians shout their signal:
        Ho! Ardsley to the van!

Give them the grave of honour where their native river ran,
Let them rest! They died like heroes
        In the battle's fiery van!

 And when their names are uttered, this hope may cheer each man:
That land shall never perish
        Where such true hearts led the van!

The aged halls of Girnington echoed to this heroic song,
and a few notes even strayed through the open windows of
the drawing-room into the twilight park. It was still evening.
A heaven unclouded smiled to the ascent of a moon un-
dimmed. That summer day was gone, and while the burning
west closed its gates upon her departure, softer paths opened
in the east for the steps of a mild summer night.

Is that horseman thinking of the glory which smiles above
those trees through which his form glances so fast? Pressing
up the avenue, he never turns to look from what source
stream those silver rays which fall upon him at every opening
of the giant boughs. Yet no heavy care absorbs his thoughts,

for he lifts his head to listen when that music comes across his way, and he smiles when at its close a laugh is heard from the mansion at whose door he now dismounts.

General and Lady Thornton sat vis à vis in two opposite arm-chair[s] by a window of their saloon. The softening light stole upon Julia, and in Sir Wilson's eyes made her look like an angel. In the background, and almost lost in the dusk, a third person sat at the piano, playing and talking at the same time. The voice sufficiently indicated her identity. It was Miss Moore, of Kirkham Lodge, Hartford, who had accompanied Colonel Thornton according to his invitation.

'General,' she was saying, in answer to some bantering speech of the worthy Baronet's, 'I am afraid I shall die an old maid.'

'I[t]'ll be your own fault if you do, I think, Jane.'

'Well, but nobody ever made me an offer yet, positively.'

'Because you're so proud and saucy,' said Julia. 'You frighten them away.'

'Indeed, you're mistaken! There's one man, at least, whom I've done my very best to win.'

'Who is that?'

'Lord Hartford. Now, I've long been in love with that man. Seriously, there's nobody I should like half so well to be married to – and I've danced with him and smiled at him and sung him all my most triumphant songs in my finest style, without as yet gaining even an outwork of the fortress. Once I thought I had made some little impression. It was after singing that Ardsley song you've heard just now. He came and stood behind me, and asked for it again. The same night, he offered to let me have his carriage to go home, for our own was engaged with my father in one of his circuits; and the next morning he actually walked down to the Lodge to breakfast with me. How I did exert myself to please! I'm sure I was most fascinating! He went home, and I fully expected to receive a proposal in form before night; but no. I'm afraid I had overshot the mark. At any rate, nothing came of it.'

'The Earl of Stuartville,' said a servant, opening the door, and the Earl of Stuartville walked in.

'Good evening, Thornton,' said his lordship. 'All in shadow, I see – no candles. Perfectly romantic! Is that Lady Julia, covered with moonlight? Good heavens! My heart's gone! Who ever saw anything so perfectly transcendent? Thornton, you'd better challenge me forthwith!'

The Earl threw himself into a chair next to Lady Julia, and, stretching out one elegant leg, leaned towards her like an enamoured Frenchman.

'What on earth has brought you here, Castlereagh?' said her ladyship. 'Excuse me for forgetting the new title – but you know, Castle, that former name must be endeared to me, for with it are connected all our earliest associations.'

'Of the days when your ladyship's pet-cognomen for me was man-monkey.'

'Happy days, those, Castlereagh!' sighed Julia. 'You'd nothing then to do but to dress and dance and dine. No Secretary of State, no General of Division business, no county politics to control or court intrigues to counteract.'

'True, Lady Julia; I used to turn out of bed at two o'clock

in the afternoon, dress till four, lounge till seven, dine till nine, and dance till six next morning.'

'You did, my dear lord; that was just a chart of your life. Alas! did I ever think the owner of the pretties[t] fancy waist-coat and the best perfumed pair of mustaches in Verdopolis would ever expose his elegance to the rigours of a winter campaign, his eye-glass to the danger of being broken in a field of battle!'

Here the chat was hushed, lost in a solemn burst of music from the piano and the reveille of a thrilling voice.

Deep the Cirhala flows,
And Evesham o'er it swells,
The last night she shall smile upon
In silence round her dwells!

All lean upon their spears,
All rest within, around,
But some shall know to-morrow night
A slumber far more sound!

The summer dew unseen
On fort and turret shines:
What dew shall fall when battle's voice
Is heard along the lines?

Trump and triumphant drum
The conflict won shall spread:
Who then will turn aside and say
We mourn the noble dead?

> Strong hands, heroic hearts
> Shall homeward throng again,
> Returned from battle's bloody grasp:
> Where will they leave the slain?
>
> Beneath a foreign sod,
> Beside an alien wave,
> Watched by the martyr's holy God,
> Who guards the martyr's grave!

Miss Moore rose and came forward as she concluded the song.

'Now, my lord,' said she, addressing the Earl of Stuartville. 'You see, I have forced you to hear, if you will not see me. Don't apologize! I am offended, of course. It will avail you nothing to say you did not observe me, it was dark, etc. You should have perceived my presence by instinct.'

'What!' returned his lordship. 'I suppose the Rose of Zamorna ought to be known by its fragrance. Miss Jane, sit down. I have something to tell you; something which – I can answer for it – will make your heart beat high with indignation.'

'Does it relate to the reason which has brought you here?' she asked, taking her seat on an ottoman near him.

'Exactly so; and you must needs think it an important circumstance which should bring me ten miles at this time of night.'

'Why then, let's hear it, without any more ado,' interposed

Thornton. 'Did aught go wrong at the magistrates' meeting after I left them?'

'No,' returned the Earl, 'except that Edward Percy and I had some sparring about a case of illegitimacy. However, that was all settled; we'd cleared scores, and Edward was just turning down his final glass of brandy and water, when Sydenham, who was standing by the court-house window, remarked that there seemed to be a crowd collecting at the lower end of the street – and as he spoke we heard a yell just for all the world like one of their election cries. I desired Mackay to go immediately and see what there was to do, but before he could get out five or six gentlemen of Zamorna rushed in a body up the steps of the magistrates' room, and the foremost announced, with more glee than grief, he believed there was going to be a riot. "What about?" I asked. Nobody answered, and some of us turned pale, for all at once a great rush thundered up the street, and in two minutes the whole front of Stancliffe's and the court-house was blocked up by a mass of howling ragamuffins.'

'Did they break t' windows?' asked Thornton.

'Not they; there was not a stone thrown, and indeed, they were not thinking of us. Their faces were all turned the other way, lifted up to the front windows of the hotel. They were yelling terribly, but for my life I could not tell what they said. However, you may be sure we set sharply about the business of swearing in special constables, and a message was despatched to the barracks to have the soldiers ready. Meantime I and Percy went out onto the steps and shouted to the crowd to disperse, but they answered us with a loud roar of "Down with Northangerland! No French! No Ardrahians!" "Well, my lads," I said, "Do you call us French? Do you say we're for Northangerland and Ardrah? If that be all, I'll join you in a hearty groan against all three – and then disperse, and go home quietly." And so the groan was given, and a tremendous rumble it was; and Edward, stepping forward and sticking his thumbs in the armholes of his waistcoat, shouted out, "Now, lads, let's have a yell – the highest you can raise – set apart entirely in honour of the old harlot-ridden buck Northangerland! Lift it up, lads! I'll set the time!" He did so, and the very steps he stood on quaked to the hellish sound they raised in unison. "Fellow-countrymen!" said Edward. "I'm proud to see such a spirit amongst you! Now go home. You've done enough for one day." But they did not stir. They only answered by a confused and horrible jabber which it was impossible to comprehend, and still they looked up at the hotel, as if there was something there they could have liked to have gotten out. "Do you think Northangerland is at Stancliffe's?" I asked. "No, no," was the answer. "We'd have had blood if he were!" and a single voice added, "But that dog, his son-in-law, is.'"

Castlereagh paused. This announcement included much. Thornton started from his chair, and strode once or twice through the room; Julia looked troubled, and uttered some faint exclamation; as for Miss Moore, she said nothing, but even in the pale moonlight it might be seen that she coloured. The Earl went on.

'When we heard this, Edward Percy just walked back into

the court-house, sat down, and said he wished he might die if he lifted a hand to prevent any thing that might happen. I stood over him and swore in good earnest, "If what we had heard was true, and if the crowd did not disperse immediately, I'd have three hundred cavalry from the barracks and ride them down like vermin." "By God you shall not," said Edward. "The soldiers have no right to control the people, d—d red tyrants!" I said my measures should be vigorous and that I would not be restrained by his cursed malignity. I got on horseback and dashed through the crowd over the way to Stancliffe's. I went in. They were all in some panic, as you may suppose, but I sent for the mistress and asked her if the Duke was really here. She said no, but that the Earl of Richton's carriage had arrived an hour ago, and that had given rise to the rumour. I asked her if the ambassador were in it, but she said, only his family physician, Dr Morrison, who had brought word that his grace had left Selden House and would be in Zamorna to-morrow at twelve o'clock. Richton was travelling with him, and Morrison preceded them by a day's journey to prepare the way. Furnished with this information, I went out again, told the people to go now and be sure to come to the same spot at noon to-morrow, when Zamorna would be there to meet them in the body. "And then," I said, "let us see what you'll do. At present he's two hundred miles off." They took the word, and in a few hours the street was clear. Now, Thornton, what think you of the prospect? You and I must be at Stancliffe's betimes in the morning. As for Edward Percy, he says he'll lie in bed all the day to-morrow.'

'Let him lie there and be d—d!' muttered Thornton. 'I care naught about him, and t' Duke deserves what he's like to get. He sudn't vex folk so. What need had he to go three or four-hundred mile to see an ow'd worn out rake? Edward's raight enow abâat that. He's allus brewing bitter drink for hisseln, and now he mun sup it for aught I know. I wish he'd his raight wit. Where's Hartford?'

'Just returned to the Hall from Gazemba. But he'll be of no use. He'll go to bed too.'

'I niver knew sich bother,' continued the worthy General. 'I hate t' thoughts o' folk being ridden down wi' troopers. It's not natural like. But if they mess wi' them they sudn't do, I care n't if t' cannon be pointed at 'em. Hasaiver ya mun flay 'em first Castlereagh – flay 'em first and let's hear what *he* says hisseln when he comes. Happen if he once gets among 'em they'll think better on't.'

'I hope they will,' echoed Julia, wringing her hands. 'I hope they will. Do you think, Thornton, they'll try to do him harm?'

'Who cares?' answered Sir William gruffly.

'I am sure you do,' said she, 'for all you're so cross about it.'

'Julia, be quiet!' returned he.

Julia was quiet; and Miss Moore looked at her from under the dark shadow of her eyelashes with an expression almost of scorn – a momentary expression which vanished instantly.

'The Duke will pass Girnington gates on his way to the city,' she observed in an indifferent tone.

'Yes,' said Castlereagh. 'But you will hardly distinguish the carriage if you watch for it. It is quite a plain one, like any private gentleman's with six horses and three postillions.'

'Perhaps one might distinguish the Duke himself,' she replied, regarding Castlereagh with the same side-glance out of the corner of her eye.

'Jane, talk sense!' said Thornton testily, and she raised her head and fixed on him a look kindling with sudden astonishment and anger. But she did not speak, and by biting in her under-lip seemed to control the emotion which was darkening her face with crimson. Thornton now asked Lord Stuartville to step with him into his study, and the party broke up.

Charles Townshend watches Zamorna's return to Zamorna City

All business seemed suspended on the morning of the 26th of June. A spirit of excitement pervaded the population of Zamorna, as though at the time of a general election. Few ladies were to be seen in the streets, but groups of gentlemen or mechanics loitered by every lamp-post. Most of the mills were idle, for the men would not come to their work. At ten o'clock the court-house doors were thrown open, and, contrary to Lord Stuartville's prediction, Lord Hartford's carriage was the first that drew up at the steps below. Special constables began to appear, leaving the magistrates' room and crossing the street to Stancliffe's. As noon approached, the crowd thickened. A dense mass began to form in front of the hotel.

It was now that from a window in the second story I saw the whole. It was a fine day – the sun burning high, the sky of its deepest summer azure – but nobody seemed to feel the scorching heat. Harried expectation appeared in every face. This would have been a capital position for a stranger, for the greatest men of the province crossed the street at every instant. General Thornton, I saw, had arrived, for he was standing on the inner steps, and pointing out to Mr Walker, a principal mill owner, a heavy red flag which hung stirless from a tall banner-staff held by two grimy operatives just opposite. As the flag occasionally deployed its sullen folds, rather to the swaying of its pole than to any breeze felt in the sultry air, it revealed these words: 'Angria scorns Traitors – Northangerland to the block'; on the reverse: 'No Percy influence'. Lord Stuartville walked up, and I heard him say distinctly, 'We'll not put down that banner! It has a good motto.' Indeed, it was evident that the nobility and gentry of the town were by no means at war with the lower orders. On the contrary, they were pleased with this demonstration of feeling against the arch-enemy, whose stinging insults were fresh in the memory and keen in the hearts of each. They only wished to keep this feeling within bounds to prevent any unseemly and impolitic ebullition.

Well, time passed on. The tumult swelled and the crowd thickened. The who[le] air seemed hoarse with sound. Impatient expectation was at its height. People looked up to the town-clock, which shewed, in vivid sunlight, its hand on the stroke of twelve: another second, and every ear heard the deep, strong stroke of iron reverberate on the air. From

Trinity Church and the minster it pealed more musically. Their chime was hardly hushed, when a few flags on the farthest outskirts of the crowd were seen to wave agitatedly. They crowded forward, and then were hurried back. A wild, deepening sound arose. One felt a sensation of panic, as it rushed on through the swaying, agitated ranks, gathering strength in its rapid approach. At last, close under the hotel windows, 'He is coming – he is coming!' was shouted from a hundred voices. Within the house the announcement rose, and footsteps stamped up the staircase. My chamber door burst open, and twenty persons were at my back, pressing one behind another to get a glimpse from the window; I saw, as I leaned far out, every sash along the wide front similarly occupied.

The magistrates were all now out on the court-house steps. I looked for Edward Percy, but doubtless he was in bed; at any rate he was not there. Meantime, a dark furrow opened in the crowded distance – I know not how, for the street had seemed too densely packed to admit another man. Slowly wading through, I perceived the heads of horses and the mounted figures of postillions. At this moment, the groan began – the scornful, abhorrent, malignant groan of the populace. It filled one with dread – the sound grew so loud and furious, the people thronged and swayed with such frantic motion, while above them the two gigantic standard bearers wildly waved their vast and gory ensign. All, meantime, stretched to gaze at the approaching carriage. It delved its way through the solid mass with difficulty, but still on it came. The horses tossed their heads high as they backed to the hard curb of the postillions. They were now near. My strained eyes viewed the whole distinctly. The carriage was open and large: it contained three figures. There was a deep interest in watching these three, and trying to discover how their present situation affected them.

One, in a white hat and blue frogged dress coat, was bending forwards and directing the postillions earnestly. He seemed anxious, I thought, for the carriage to be drawn up close by the court-house; he looked towards the gentlemen there, and glances of intelligence seemed to pass between them and him. These – I mean the magistrates – had all uncovered. Lord Stuartville appeared in front; his curls were shining in the sun; he held his hat in one hand and with the other was motioning to the people to part their ranks. General Thornton, likewise hat in hand, was hastily giving orders to [a] man whom I knew to be his own attendant; I saw him point to the barracks. As to Lord Hartford, he stood back silent and upright: his deep eye wandered over the people and fixed fiercely on the carriage. Lord Richton (of course the owner of the blue frogged coat and white hat could be no other) is said not to have the nerves of a lion, yet he can exhibit much self-possession in cases of considerable apparent danger. I was amused by watching the calmness of his face, divested either of smile or frown and expressing in its light eyes, always quick in their motions, a sort of concern wholly unmixed with either fear or anger. He seemed to take upon himself the office of dictator and manager, and very busy he appeared, now telegraphing with the group on the court-house steps, and now checking or urging the postillions as prudence seemed to demand. The other male occupant of the carriage was very still. He leaned back in what seemed a very careless posture; a hat with a broad brim and slouched much forwards shaded his face; he said nothing; he looked at nobody. The only token of life I saw him give was taking a gold snuff-box from his waistcoat pocket, tapping it thrice, extracting a pinch of snuff with his finger and thumb, then replacing the box and buttoning his coat well over it.

A more interesting object was presented by the third figure of this group – a lady, and, of course, the Duchess of Zamorna. She was dressed with that sort of stylish simplicity peculiar to herself – a light summer pelisse, gracefully fitted to her figure; a pretty simple bonnet, tyed with a broad ribbon; no veil, no flower, no plume. Her very hair was smoothed out of its native luxuriance of curl, and plainly parted on her forehead: this mode, which suits so few, suited her. It seemed to impart additional serenity to her forehead, additional straightness and delicacy to her nose; it reli[e]ved by more striking contrast her fair, transparent complexion, and gave her eyes a touch of something saintly. I cannot tell whether she was afraid, or grieved or mortified; your great people will not reveal their emotions to the eyes of common men; however, she was wholly colourless except a faint tinge in the lips.

'No Percy influence!' shouted and howled the frantic mob. 'Down with Northangerland – roll his bloody head in the dirt!' and they shook the insulting banner high over his daughter, involving her figure for a moment in the sullen fiery shade reflected from its folds. Meantime, the person in the broad

63

brim sat like any wet Quaker whom the spirit had not yet moved. His carriage, however, having by dint of Richton's skilful pilotage at length reached the court-house, now cast anchor at the steps, the cessation of motion seemed to remind him that he was in rather a peculiar situation. He gave a look straight before him, then to the right hand, the left, and finally over his shoulder. After a moment's meditation he lifted his forefinger and beckoned to the Earl of Stuartville. I was surprised to see him do anything half so intelligent. A conference of three minutes ensued, in which Stuartville's part seemed to consist in answering a string of running questions delivered as fast as the lips of the inquirer could move. Broad-brim then drew himself up, lifted his beaver a little, rose all at once to his feet in the carriage, and in so doing uncovered his head. A breeze passing through his hair waved it from temples and brow. He stood confessed.

A sudden movement, unexpected, generally checks affairs, for a moment at least, in whatever channel they may chance to be running. On the present occasion, this rising of the Duke of Zamorna lulled the yell which had given him such hoarse welcome to his kingdom. The hush first dropped on those immediately round him; others caught the feeling that there was something to be seen, something to be heard, and they too were silent. The calm spread, and ere long nothing was to be heard but the dull ocean-murmur of a mighty and expectant multitude. He, meantime, remained erect, the breast of his coat open, one hand resting on his side. The other at first held his hat, till Richton relieved him of it without his apparently being conscious it was gone. He seemed to wait and watch till the living vortex round him sunk into tranquillity. Comparative silence stole over it: every eye sought his. So mute was the pause of expectation, one's heart quaked at the thought of its being broken.

'I wish,' said the Duke of Zamorna, 'I wish, lads, you'd all something to do at home.'

His voice was familiar, and so were his features. The people seemed disposed to hear more, and, after pushing his long fingers through his hair, he spoke again.

'Is there a man among you wise enough to render a reason for the bonny display you're making just now?'

('Yes! Yes!' exclaimed several voices.)

'I say no! Is it because I have been to see an old acquaintance and distant relative of mine who is a feeble invalid?'

('Your Grace has been taking on wi' Northangerland again and we hate him,' replied a single voice in the crowd.)

'What do you say, my lad?' said the Duke, who, it seems, had not distinctly heard the observation. The man repeated it.

'Taking on with Northangerland!' continued his Grace. 'That's a vague sort of expression. I've been to the south, looking after my own and my kinsfolk's concerns, and concerning myself no more about politics than most of you do about religion.'

'Have you leagued with Northangerland?' asked one of the bannermen sternly.

The Duke turned upon him with a dark and changed aspect. He eyed his rebellious standard and said coldly, 'Take down that flag.'

'No!' shouted the bannerman. 'This is the flag of the people.'

'Take it down,' replied his Grace in a deepened tone, and he savagely glared at the magistrates. They instantly despatched six special constables to execute the Duke's mandate. Loud uproar ensued; the huge flag was tossed up and down as its bearers struggled to retain what the constables were resolved to seize; the yelling of the mob redoubled; and all at once, with hideous roar, a rush was made on the royal carriage. A frightful scene ensued. The gentlemen who had crowded the court-house steps and windows sprang into the crowd. A dismal shriek was heard as the startled horses – no longer obedient to the postillions – plunged in terror amongst the densely wedged crowd. Their wild eyes and streaming manes were seen tossed over the sea of human heads, as their iron hoofs, prancing madly, crushed all around them. I looked in agony at the Duchess; she was bending back, and had hid her face in the cushions of the carriage. As for Zamorna, with teeth fast set and the curls of his bare head shadowing his fierce eyes, he looked hellish; he gave not a word either to his wife or Lord Richton; his glance was fixed in one direction. At last, as a thundering beating sound and a dense cloud of dust rose in the quarter where he looked, he got up, and speaking with a very loud distinct voice said,

'Men of Zamorna, three hundred horsemen are upon you. I see them; they are here; you will be ridden down in five minutes if you do not bear back instantly from the carriage.' There was no time: with horse-hair waving and broad sabres glancing, with loud huzza and dint of thunder, the cavalry charged on the mob. Lord Stuartville led the van, waving his hat and mounted on a horse like a devil. Nothing could stand this, not even the mad mechanics and desperate operatives of Zamorna. They flew like chaff; it was the whirlwind chasing the sand of the desert. Causeway and carriage were cleared; the wide street lay bare in the fierce sun behind them. A few wounded men alone were left with shattered limbs, lying on the pavement. These were soon taken off to the infirmary, their blood was washed from the stones, and no sign remained of what had happened. When I looked for the royal carriage, it stood in front of Stancliffe's, empty; a cloak was flung over the seat and two grooms were taking out the horses. *Sic transit etc.*

Sir William Percy describes Zamorna's anger at the city leaders

It was afternoon, and the hotel was somewhat quieter. I had gone out to get a little cool air in the garden, whose bushy shrubs in some measure screened the sun. Two or three gentlemen were walking there, and in an arbour I found Sir William Percy.

'Well, Colonel, where did you put yourself this morning while that dust was kicking up?'

'O, I got the snuggest possible corner in the court-house. I witnessed the whole spectacle quite at my ease. Very good sport for winter; rather too active for these dog-days. How the canaille did run! What will your brother say when he hears of their rout?'

'Bah – swear himself to the bottomless pit and then call for a drop of brandy to cool his tongue! But Townshend, don't I look very languid? quite stived up, to use a classical phrase?'

'Can't say but you do. The heat seems to have overpowered you.'

'Well it may. Ever since noon, I've been in the presence of the Great Mogul.'

'What, of Zamorna?'

'No other. He sent for a whole lot of us into the great dining room; and then, when I and Stuartville and Thornton and Sydenham and Walker and a dozen more went in, he was striding up and down from the fire-place to the window with a face ten times blacker than the smoke from Edward's tobacco-pipe. He just stood and put his hand on the long table when we came in, each man doffing his castor and bowing at the door. He never asked us to sit down, but let us stand at the lower end, like four and twenty honey-pots all of a row. He began by asking Lord Stuartville if the troops were gone back to their quarters. Stuartville stept forward a pace and made answer that they were, with the exception of a small detachment which had been left to keep order in a part of the town which as yet seemed scarcely settled. "Then," his grace continued, as coldly as you please, "I must say, my lord, I have been a good deal surprised at the state of dissatisfaction in which I have found the province under your lieutenancy." And without softening this pretty sentence by another word he stopped for an answer.

'Stuartville said very plainly, "he believed there was a strong feeling in the minds of the people against the Earl of

Northangerland." "Allow me to put your meaning in other words," said His Grace. "There seems to me to be a strong feeling in the minds of the people that they have a right to dictate how, when, where, to whom and on what subject they will. Let it be your business, and that of the gentlemen behind you, to subdue this feeling; to shew those who entertain it the fallacy and danger of acting upon it." General Thornton remarked that they had done their best, he thought, that morning. The answer he received proved to him that this idea was all a delusion. "I have not seen your conduct in that light," said the Mogul. "Ordinary vigilance on the part of the city authorities would have prevented the assemblage of such a mass of scum. Ordinary decision would have broken into firewood the staff of that banner which in your town was this day insolently hoisted over my head." He made another of his frozen pauses, and then asked if the Mayor of Zamorna was present. Mr Maude bowed and came forward. "Your police is lax," began His Grace without a word of civility. "Your Corporation is indolent, and ought to be overhauled. Every thing indicates disorder, negligence and misrule. If I do not find a speedy change for the better, I shall consider it my duty to set on foot measures for depriving your city of its corporate privileges."

'There fell another pause, in the course of which Mr Sydenham said "he believed His Grace judged the town too hardly. It was his opinion that the feeling manifested that day was no proof of disloyalty, but the contrary." At this speech the Duke scowled like a Saracen. Fixing his eyes on Sydenham he said, "Favour me by keeping that opinion to yourself while you remain in this room. I never yet admitted the value of the loyalty which would dictate the choice of my private friends, or control the course of my private actions. It was not on that condition I accepted the crown of Angria – and how long will it take you to learn that when I became a monarch I did not cease to be a man? Your country put into my hands the splendour and power of royalty, but I did not offer in exchange the freedom and independence of private life." Nobody answered him and, after another of his pauses, he began dictating again. "Lord Stuartville, Zamorna has not done well under your Lieutenancy. In this capacity you have disappointed my expectations. I must supersede you if you do not act with greater vigour." Stuartville coloured high and said, much moved, "Your Grace shall be anticipated. From this moment I resign my office. Had I been aware before –." And, would you believe it, Townshend, here he broke off with a gulp as if he had been choked. Thornton went red too and said he thought all this was far too bad. Our Czar went on: "Your magistracy have disgraced themselves; one was absent; another was perfectly inactive; and the remaining four shewed neither foresight, resolution, nor energy. Gentlemen, you may go." And so he turned his back on us, walked up to the window, and we made our exit. Thornton's gone back to Girnington as surly as a bull; Stuartville flung himself on his break-neck horse and set off at a gallop, which must have brought him to the D—l long since; Sydenham and Walker both mounted the Edwardston stage and are doubtless now drinking d—tion to the sovereign in a bumper of Edward's best; as for me, I came here to take the air and get an appetite for some fricandeau[25] I've just ordered.'

'Well,' said I. 'There's a pretty go! And pray, what has become of the Duchess? Do you know whether she's frightened to death?'

'Almost, I daresay. She did look white when the rush began; I heard she turned sick as soon as they got her into Stancliffe's.'

'Then you've not seen her?'

'Yes, for a minute; going up the staircase leaning on Richton's arm.'

'Did you speak?'

'No. Indeed, she was all but dead then, and neither noticed me nor anybody else. The man is coming to say my fricandeau is ready. Townshend, will you walk in and take a snack?'

Zamorna and his wife Mary at Stancliffe's Hotel

Evening drew on at length. Oh, how cool, how balmy its first breeze came sighing, to call away the beams of day-light. Sunset was over; the streets were still and dim; an early moon gazed from heaven on the towers of Zamorna's minster, which fairly lifted its white front and shafted oriel to meet that gaze. The breeze which ushers in evening fluttered the blinds of a large upper saloon at Stancliffe's. Every window was shaded, as if to shut out light and noise and all that could chase repose from that couch in the recess. Sunk among a pile of cushions, a lady lies asleep – pale, with her hair loose, and

71

her figure shewing in its attitude the relaxation of extreme fatigue.

Is that person about to awake her, who is leaning over the couch? Pity there is not another living soul in the room to bid him stand away, and let her sleep! What is the individual smiling at? He seems to find matter for amusement in the exhaustion of that slender form and marble face, and the saintly folding of those little fairy hands. Villain, don't touch her! But with his long fore-finger he is parting the loose hair farther from her forehead, and then he smiles again at what any other person would worship – the open brow, gleaming fair and serene like that of a sculptured Virgin Mary. He takes his unhallowed hands from her for a moment, and puts them in his pocket. Man, you look no fit guardian for that shrine! You break the harmony of the scene. Why don't you go away? All round is so still and dim, and she is so fair, one might think her a saint and this room a consecrated chapel. But while you stand there I defy anybody to soothe their mind with so pious a delusion: a fellow with whiskers and something like mustaches, and so much hair – almost black it looks in this light – that you hardly know whether he has any forehead or not, until all at once he pushes the pile away and then there's an expanse underneath, whose smoothness tells you he's not old enough to be a priest.

Fresh from the stern interview with his Lord Lieutenant and the Corporation, from scenes of an equally iron nature which had followed and occupied him all the afternoon, Zamorna had now sought, in the cool of evening, the apartment to which his Duchess had retired. It was an undefined

72

mixture of feelings that brought him there. Half, he wished to know how she had borne the scene of the morning – a scene so unfitted to her nature. Half, he felt an inclination to repose on her softness faculties worried with the bitter and angry contest of the day. Then, in metaphysical indistinctness, existed, scarce known to himself, the consciousness that it was her connection with him which had thus embroiled him with his people; and he was come now partly to please himself with her beauty, partly to dream away an hour in amiable meditations on the sorcery of female charms and the peril of doating on them too fondly, being guided by them too implicitly.

He drew aside the crimson curtain and let the evening sun shine upon her. He walked softly to and fro in the saloon, and every time he passed her couch turned on her his ardent gaze. That man has now loved Mary Percy longer than he ever loved any woman before, and I daresay her face has by this time become to him a familiar and household face. It may be told, by the way in which his eye seeks the delicate and pallid features and rests on their lines, that he finds settled pleasure in the contemplation. In all moods, at all times, he likes them. Her temper is changeful; she is not continual sunshine; she weeps sometimes, and frets and teazes him not unfrequently with womanish jealousies. I don't think another woman lives on earth in whom he would bear these changes for a moment. From her, they almost please him. He finds an amusement in playing with her fears – piquing or soothing them as caprice directs.

She slept still, but now he stoops to wake her. He separated her clasped hands and took one in his own. Disturbed by the movement, she drew that hand hastily and petulantly away, and turned on her couch with a murmur. He laughed, and the laugh woke her. Rising, she looked at him and smiled. Still she seemed weary, and when he placed himself beside her she dropped her head on his shoulder and would have slept again. But the Duke would not permit this: he was come for his evening's amusement, and his evening's amusement he would have, whether she was fit to yield it or not. In answer to his prohibitory and disturbing movements she said,

'Adrian, I am tired.'

'Too tired to talk to me?' he asked.

'No, Adrian, but let me lean against you.'

Still he held her off.

'Come,' said he. 'Open your eyes and fasten your hair up; it is hanging on your neck like a mermaid's.' The Duchess raised her hand to her hair; it was indeed all loose and dishevelled over her shoulders. She got up to arrange it, and the occupation roused her. Having smoothed the auburn braids before a mirror, and touched and retouched her loosened dress till it resumed its usual aspect of fastidious neatness, she walked to the window.

'The sun is gone,' said she. 'I am too late to see it set.' And she pensively smiled as her eye lingered on the soft glory which the sun, just departed, had left in its track. 'That is the West!' she exclaimed; and, turning to Zamorna, added quickly, 'What if you had been born a great imaginative Angrian?'

'Well, I should have played the fool as I have done by marrying a little imaginative Senegambian.'

'And,' she continued, talking half to herself and half to him, 'I should have had a very different feeling towards you then to what I have now. I should have fancied you cared nothing about my country so far off, with its wide wild woodlands. I should have thought all your heart was wrapt in this land, so fair and rich, teeming with energy and life, but still, Adrian, not with the romance of the West.'

'And what do you think now, my Sappho?'

'That you are not a grand awful foreigner absorbed in your kingdom as the grandest land of the earth, looking at me as an exotic, listening to my patriotic rhapsodies as sentimental dreams, but a son of Senegambia as I am a daughter – a thousand times more glorious to me, because you are the most glorious thing my own land ever flung from her fire-fertilized soil! I looked at you when those Angrians were howling round you today, and remembered that you were my countryman, not theirs – and all at once their alien senses, their foreign hearts, seemed to have discerned something uncongenial in you, the great stranger, and they rose under your control, yelling rebelliously.'

'Mary!' exclaimed the Duke, laughingly approaching her. 'Mary, what ails you this evening? Let me look – is it the same quiet little winsome face I am accustomed to see?' He raised her face and gazed but she turned with a quick movement away.

'Don't, Adrian. I have been dreaming about Percy Hall. When will you let me go there?'

'Any time. Set off to-night if you please.'

'That is nonsense, and I am serious. I must go sometime – but you never let [me] do anything I wish.'

'Indeed! You dared not say so, if you were not far too much indulged.'

'Let me go, and come with me in about a month when you have settled matters at Adrianopolis – promise, Adrian.'

'I'll let *you* go willingly enough,' returned Zamorna, sitting down and beginning to look vexatious. 'But as for asking me to leave Angria again for at least a year and a day – none but an over-fondled wife would think of preferring an unreasonable request.'

'It is not unreasonable, and I suppose you want me to leave you? I'd never allow *you* to go fifteen hundred miles if I could help it.'

'No,' returned His Grace. 'Nor fifteen hundred yards either. You'd keep me like a china ornament in your drawing-room. Come, dismiss that pet![26] What is it all about?'

'Adrian, you look so scornful.'

He took up a book which lay in the window-seat, and began to read. The Duchess stood a while looking at him, and knitting her arched and even brows. He turned over page after page, and by the composure of his brow expressed interest in what he was reading and an intention to proceed. Her Grace is by no means the victim of caprice, though now and then she seems daringly to play with weapons few besides would venture to handle. On this occasion her tact, so nice as to be infallible, informed her that the pet was carried far enough. She sat down, then, by Zamorna's side; leant over and looked at the book; it was poetry – a volume of Byron. Her attention, likewise, was arrested; and she continued to read, turning the page with her slender [finger], after looking into the Duke's face at the conclusion of each leaf to see if he was ready to proceed. She was so quiet, her hair so softly fanned his cheek as she leaned her head towards him, the contact of her gentle hand now and then touching his, of her smooth and silken dress, was so endearing, that it quickly appeased the incipient ire her whim of perverseness had raised; and when, in about half an hour, she ventured to close the obnoxious volume and take it from his hand, the action met with no resistance – nothing but a shake of the head, half-reproving, half-indulgent.

Little more was said by either Duke or Duchess, or at least their further conversation was audible to no mortal ear. The shades of dusk were gathering in the room; the very latest beam of sunset was passing from its gilded walls. They sat in the deep recess of the window side by side, a cloudless moon looking down from the sky upon them and lighting their faces with her smile. Mary leant her happy head on a breast she thought she might trust – happy in that belief, even though it were a delusion. Zamorna had been kind, even fond, and, for aught she knew, faithful, ever since their last blissful meeting at Adrianopolis, and she had learnt how to rest in his arms with a feeling of security, not trembling lest when she most needed the support it might all at once be torn away. During their late visit to Northangerland he had shewn her marked attention, conscious that tenderness bestowed on her was the surest method of soothing her father's heart, and words could not express half the rapture of her feelings when, more than once, seated between the Earl and Duke on such an evening as this, she had perceived that both regarded her as the light and hope of their lives. Language had not revealed this to her. Her father is a man of few words on sentimental matters; her husband, of none at all, though very vigorous in his actions; but Northangerland cheered in her presence, and Zamorna watched her from morning till night, following all her movements with a keen and searching glance.

Is that Hannah Rowley tapping at the door? She says tea is [ready], and Mr Surena impatient to get into the shop again. Goodbye, reader.

June 28th 1838

Notes

1. *exercised*: Conducted the service, expounded scripture (obsolete).
2. *Rossland*: Ross's Land, the kingdom founded by Captain John Ross, Anne Brontë's principal character in the Young Men's Play.
3. *adipose*: Fat. Apparently this is a comic substitution for 'comatose': Macara is not yet in command of language.
4. *news-room*: In the 1830s, a reading-room set aside for the reading of newspapers.
5. *ascent*: Eminence (obsolete).
6. *nankeens*: Trousers made of a kind of cotton cloth.
7. *market-fresh*: Slang for drunk, referring to 'that dubious degree of sobriety with which farmers too commonly return home from market' (1841; *Oxford English Dictionary*).
8. *pea-surtouts*: Stout overcoats made of coarse cloth.
9. *jobation*: Talking to.
10. *fire-eater*: One fond of quarrelling or fighting.
11. *Olympian*: The country houses of the Angrian gentry are in the valley of the Olympian.
12. *the genuine Angrian hue*: Red.
13. *jeans*: Trousers made of coarse cotton cloth.
14. *Genii dreams*: Comic reference to the origins of Angria in Glass Town, whose creators were the Four Chief Genii.

15. *heel-tap*: The liquor left at the bottom of a glass after drinking.

16. *Giaour*: Islamic term of abuse for Christians, and title of a poem by Lord Byron (1813).

17. *endued*: Put on as a garment (*OED*); the word also has the sense of 'invest or endow with a spiritual gift', and carries a mock-heroic resonance here.

18. *carr-brake*: Fen or bog surrounded by low growth.

19. *hells*: Gambling dens.

20. *Stock*: Kind of stiff, close-fitting neckcloth.

21. *aigrette*: Spray of gems, worn on the head (from the tuft of the egret) (French).

22. *embayment*: Bay-like recess (of a window).

23. *prigging*: Thieves' cant for stealing.

24. *salmagundi*: Dish composed of chopped meat, anchovies, eggs and onions, with oil and condiments.

25. *fricandeau*: 'A slice of veal or other meat dried or stewed and served with sauce' (*OED*) (French).

26. *pet*: Temper.

CLICK ON A CLASSIC

www.penguinclassics.com

The world's greatest literature at your fingertips